NO ESCAPE

CAN ONE EVER LEAVE THEIR PAST BEHIND?

MARK DAVID ABBOTT

MARK DAVID ABBOTT

Copyright © 2019 by Mark David Abbott

All rights reserved.

No part of this book may be reproduced in any form or by any electronic or mechanical means, including information storage and retrieval systems, without written permission from the author, except for the use of brief quotations in a book review.

For the wonderful people of Oman.

DO YOU WANT ADVANCE NOTICE OF THE NEXT ADVENTURE?

The next book is currently being written, but if you sign up for my VIP newsletter I will let you know as soon as it is released.

Your email will be kept 100% private and you can unsubscribe at any time.

If you are interested, please visit my website:

www.markdavidabbott.com
(No Spam. Ever.)

1

Steve Jones checked the room number against the message on his phone, then knocked twice.

He heard a muffled "Come in" through the door and pushed down on the latch, stepping inside. A short hallway opened into a large suite with expansive views across the Arabian Gulf from the full-height windows. An older Indian man, sitting in an overstuffed leather armchair, watched him approach, and Steve smiled.

"Mr. Patil?"

"Yes," replied the man as he gestured toward another chair.

Steve nodded and walked over, taking a quick glance around the room. A polished wooden writing desk stood against one wall, and on the opposite side of the room, a set of double sliding doors opened into the bedroom. The leather armchair and sofa set arranged around a coffee table took up the center of the room. On the coffee table sat a silver tray laden with cups and a large coffee pot. Steve did a quick calculation in his head. A suite like this would cost upwards of three thousand *dirhams* a night—he made a mental note to revise his charges upwards.

"Please help yourself to coffee."

"Thank you." Steve sat down and placed his messenger bag on the floor beside the chair before pouring himself a cup. Sitting back, he smiled at the man in front of him. He was older than he sounded on the phone, perhaps in his mid-fifties, his head bald on top, and the hair at the sides grey and slicked back. The gold chain around his neck and the white linen shirt stretched over a 'prosperous' belly only reinforced the aura of wealth hinted at by the hotel suite. He frowned impatiently, his fingers tapping on the arm of the chair as Steve sipped on his coffee.

"Well?"

"Oh, yes." Steve placed the coffee cup back on the table and reached for his messenger bag, removing a notepad, flipping it open.

"He is staying in this hotel, room 1502, has been here for four days."

"His name?" Surya Patil interrupted.

Steve checked his notes. "Ah... John Hayes. Traveling on an English passport." Steve looked up and noticed his client's frown was even deeper, a vein visibly pulsing in his temple, his hands now clenched into fists. Steve looked down at his notes again, wondering what his client's connection was with the hotel guest. He had been working as a private investigator in Dubai for almost three years now, the bulk of his work monitoring the infidelities of men and women on business trips. But this case didn't seem like that.

The beautiful woman accompanying Mr. Hayes wasn't Indian, so she was obviously not a relative of his client. She didn't look like a woman who would be in a relationship with an unattractive middle-aged and overweight man either. Although he had to admit, he had seen plenty of strange relationships during his three years in the city. It was amazing what the lure of money made people do.

"And the woman?"

"A Portuguese national. Adriana D'Silva," Steve read from his notes, then looked up. "That's all I've been able to find out, so far."

Surya Patil nodded slowly, his eyes drilling holes in Steve, forcing him to look away. He placed the notepad on his lap and picked up the coffee cup, taking another sip.

"I want you to follow them. Find out where they go, what they do, who they meet. I expect a report."

"Of course," Steve smiled. He glanced around the suite again. "Ah... there will be expenses, and of course, you know my daily rate."

Surya Patil's lip curled in distaste as he leaned forward and picked up an envelope from the coffee table.

"Consider this an advance." He tossed it over the table into Steve's lap.

Steve placed the cup down and picked up the envelope, flicking it open with his thumb, and glanced at the thick wad of *dirhams* inside. Looking up, he smiled.

"Perfect."

Surya Patil dismissed him with a wave of his hand, and Steve retrieved his bag and stood up. He nodded goodbye but needn't have bothered. Surya Patil was staring out the window, ignoring him.

Steve turned and walked toward the door, the cash-stuffed envelope safely stowed in his bag. It had come at an opportune time. The last two months had been lean, and he was behind on the alimony payments to his wife back in Australia. He didn't understand what this Surya Patil wanted with the Englishman and his partner, but as long as he kept paying, he would do whatever he asked.

He reached for the door handle, opening the door when Surya Patil's gruff voice called out from behind him.

"A daily report. Don't forget!"

Steve smiled to himself. "Of course, Sir. I'll call you first thing tomorrow morning."

2
———

Detective Inspector Rajiv Sampath closed the file on his desk and added it to the ever-growing pile to his right. Rubbing his face with his hands, he sat back in his chair. It had been a long boring morning. The paperwork in his job never seemed to end; in fact, it seemed to be increasing—countless reports and red tape. Every time a new Home Minister was appointed, he had to start all over again. There seemed to be little time left for actual policing. He sighed. He needed coffee.

"Paramshiva?" he called out and waited until the constable poked his head around the door frame.

"Sir?"

"Get me a coffee, will you?"

"Yes, Sir."

"Oh, and Paramshiva, less sugar, please."

"Yes, sir," the constable smiled and disappeared from the door.

Rajiv sighed and ran his hand down over his midsection. All this desk work was making him fat. He prided himself on maintaining his fitness as an example to his men, and the overly sweetened coffee served in the station wasn't helping matters.

He reached for another file and opened it, scanning the contents, and shook his head. One more file, then he was leaving the office. He needed to get out, patrol the streets, check on his men.

He was halfway through the file when the constable returned with a stainless-steel tumbler filled with steaming hot coffee. Placing it on the desk in front of Rajiv, he waited until he looked up.

"What is it, Paramshiva?"

"Sir, a call came in for you." He handed over a piece of paper with a number on it. "Patil, Sir, he wants you to call him back."

Rajiv frowned. "Me? Are you sure he doesn't want the boss?"

"Yes, Sir. He asked for you."

"Okay," Rajiv nodded thoughtfully. "Thank you."

"Yes, Sir." The constable turned and left the room.

Rajiv looked at the number. It wasn't an Indian number; it started with +971—Dubai. Strange. Rajiv pursed his lips and drummed his fingers on the desktop. *I wonder what he wants with me.* Usually, these politicians only spoke to his boss, S.P.I Muniappa, and Rajiv preferred it that way. He didn't like the constant meddling from above, preferring to devote himself to actual police work.

Rajiv had joined the force to fight crime and keep his country safe, not indulge the whims of whichever government minister was currently in power. However there was a fine line to tread when dealing with politicians. If he didn't keep them happy—within reason—it could be the death knell for his career.

He sighed and looked at his watch—mid-morning in

Dubai. Picking up the phone, he dialed—only one way to find out what the man wants.

Five minutes later, he hung up the phone and stood up. John Hayes—a name he hadn't heard for a while, not since that dreadful incident with his wife. The investigation had been handled very badly by the force, in no small way due to pressure from Surya Patil himself, and Rajiv wasn't proud of the outcome. A great injustice had been done to Mr. Hayes, and that wasn't the type of policing Rajiv stood for.

When Rajiv had waved him off at the airport all those years ago, he thought it was the last he would ever hear of him and was glad. He had never been able to prove John Hayes had taken matters into his own hands and taken revenge, but he had to admit, he secretly admired the man for doing so when the legal system had stood by and done nothing.

Now, Surya Patil himself was asking for his file. He paced around the room, his mind working out the possible connotations. No good would come of this, he was sure. Rajiv sighed, walking over to the open door.

"Paramshiva? Get me the Charlotte Hayes file. From three years ago."

3

Surya Patil leaned on the balcony handrail and gazed out over the vast expanse of sea in front of him, but his eyes didn't see the clear blue waters of the Arabian Gulf. Instead, his mind raced, searching back through his memories of events almost three years ago. A hollowness filled his chest as he remembered his son, Sunil. They hadn't got along, Sunil frequently disappointing him, but he had been his only son, and it hurt that he was no longer around. Surya ground his teeth and gripped the steel handrail, the knuckles on his hands turning white.

John Hayes—he knew he looked familiar when he watched him walk through the lobby, but it was only when the private investigator's research confirmed it, that the memories flooded back. It was a dark time. His son had denied any involvement in the death of John Hayes' wife, but Surya knew he had been behind it. He also believed John Hayes killed Sunil and his friends in retribution. The police had proved nothing despite an immense amount of pressure from him, and after John Hayes disappeared from the country, Surya resigned himself to never receiving justice—until now. It had to be fate. Why else would they be staying at the same hotel? What his son, Sunil, had done was inexcusable, but no-one, *no-one* had the right to harm Surya's family, and he would stop at nothing to get his revenge.

He heard a ping from the laptop in his suite and walked back inside to the writing desk and stared at the screen. An email had come in, a brief message with an attachment. Pulling out the chair, he sat down and stabbed at the keyboard with his fingers. He still couldn't get used to the computer. Usually one of his staff did everything for him, but on this trip, he had come alone, preferring to keep the reasons for his trip unknown—the fewer people who knew about his accounts in Dubai, the better. The last thing he wanted was for his political rivals to learn about the hidden accounts he kept offshore—accounts filled with the black money he was paid for sanctioning infrastructure projects in Bangalore and the state. They all did it, they all maintained offshore accounts, it was an open secret, but proving it was another thing.

Two days had been enough to complete his meetings with the banks, and he had been booked on the evening's flight back to Bangalore, but having spotted John Hayes, he postponed his return.

Finally, figuring out how to open the attached file, he scanned through the contents until he found the photos. He grimaced at the sight of the mutilated and battered body of Charlotte Hayes and clicked through quickly until he found a photo of John. Enlarging it until it filled the screen, he sat back in his chair and studied the photo. It was definitely the same man he had seen in the lobby, although now he looked happier, his hair a little shorter than in the photo, and his skin deeply tanned... there was no mistaking him.

Surya rubbed his face with his hands and pinched the bridge of his nose with his thumb and forefinger. He could feel pressure in his temples, and his heart was racing. He slammed the heel of his hand down on the desk. John Hayes. The murderer of his son. In his hotel. The bastard! He must take action, he couldn't let the opportunity slide. He pushed back the chair and stood up, turning to pace the room. If he was back in India, it would be easy, but here in Dubai? He didn't have the connections here, the contacts, the ready access to thugs and goons who would make someone's life a misery for a paltry number of rupees. He walked back to the desk and closed the laptop, then moved to the bar and poured himself three fingers of whiskey.

He had to do something... but what?

4

"Do you feel like a coffee?"

Adriana pulled him closer and kissed him on the side of his neck.

"Yes, let's go over there."

John smiled and led Adriana over to the café and looked for an empty table. Choosing one by the window, he pulled out a chair for Adriana and waited for her to sit down before sitting in the chair opposite.

"Ahh, it's good to sit down."

Adriana grinned back. "This mall is ridiculous. It's so big."

A young, Filipina waitress came over to the table and greeted them. "Hello, Ma'am, Sir."

"Hi, how are you?"

"Good, Sir," she replied, rolling the 'r's in Sir. "Are you having a good day?"

"Yes, we are, thank you, but I would love a coffee. One Americano and..." John looked across at Adriana. "A mocha?"

"Yes please, extra hot."

"Thank you, Ma'am, Sir, anything to eat?"

"Not right now, thank you."

The waitress smiled and walked back to the counter.

John watched her go, then turned his attention to the view outside the window. Crowds of people wandered past, western tourists in beach and leisurewear, hands filled with shopping bags or staring at their phones. Interspersed between them were the occasional Emiratis, the men in crisp white *dishdashas* and immaculately trimmed beards, the women with perfect makeup and black *abayas* covering all but the fleeting glimpse of an expensive shoe as they walked.

John looked back at Adriana, who was watching him, a bemused look on her face.

"Not a big fan of shopping, are you, Mr. Hayes?"

John gave a wry grin. "No, is it that obvious?"

"Yes," Adriana laughed, her hazel eyes sparkling with amusement. Reaching up, she tucked a stray strand of hair behind her ear. "But it's okay, neither am I. After coffee, let's get out of here, do something different."

John gazed back at her. He never tired of looking at her—her beautiful, smooth, olive skin, her cheekbones, and those eyes that sparkled with gold in the light.

The coffees arrived, and he waited until the waitress retreated before taking a sip. It was good, a little strong but good. He put the cup back down and cleared his throat.

"I've been thinking, why don't we go somewhere else? I think I've had enough of big cities for a while, and there's not much to do here apart from shopping and eating."

Adriana studied him over the rim of her coffee cup. Nodding thoughtfully, she placed the cup down on the table. John reached forward with a napkin.

"You have some milk on your lip."

Adriana dabbed her mouth and examined the napkin before replying, "John, I feel guilty."

John raised an eyebrow, "Why? About what?"

"Well..." Adriana picked up a teaspoon and played with the froth on the top of her coffee, then looked up. "Don't get me wrong, I'm having a wonderful time, but..."

"But what?" John leaned in, his forehead creased.

"You're spending all this money on me, but you won't let me pay for anything..."

"Adriana, please don't worry." John relaxed and sat back, a slow smile forming on his face. "I told you money doesn't matter. What matters is us being together, enjoying our lives." John reached forward and took her hand. "You saw what those people had gone through in the refugee camp. We are so fortunate we're not in that position. Let's make the most of it."

Adriana tilted her head to one side and was quiet for a moment before speaking.

"I understand that, but shouldn't we be doing something, instead of just enjoying ourselves? Shouldn't we be trying to make the world a better place?"

John slipped his hand away and shrugged. "Maybe." He picked up his coffee cup, took another sip, then put it down again and looked out the window.

"Adriana, before I met you, I was in a dark place. I've not told you about it yet... perhaps one day, I will." He looked back at her. "But now I've met you, I want to enjoy every moment. You've brought light back into my life..." He paused, searching for the right words. "I'm fortunate I don't have to work for a living anymore. The universe in that way has been kind to me. So, please don't worry about the money... and who knows, when the time is right, perhaps the universe will show us some direction, but right now, let's enjoy the present and let the future take care of itself."

Adriana gazed back at him for a moment before reaching across the table for his hand. "I love you, John Hayes." She gave his hand a squeeze and smiled, the corners of her eyes crinkling up. "Now, where shall we go next?"

5

Detective Inspector Rajiv Sampath leaned his butt against the hood of the Police Bolero, raised the paper cup of hot sweet *chai* to his lips, and took a sip. It had been another long day, and he needed the *chai* to keep him awake. He handed ten rupees to his driver, who walked over to the *chai wallah* and paid him. Despite being almost midnight, the *chai wallah* was doing a roaring trade, dispensing the hot *chai* from a stainless-steel urn strapped to the back of his bicycle. Rickshaw *wallahs* and taxi drivers on the night shift crowded around him, smoking and chatting, the detritus of used paper cups and cigarette butts scattered at their feet. A pair of mangy dogs prowled the perimeter, hoping for a biscuit or two.

Rajiv allowed his mind to wander and thought back to the call he had taken from Surya Patil earlier in the day. The call brought to the surface disturbing memories of the Charlotte Hayes case so many years ago. In legal terms, the result had been dissatisfying—Charlotte's assaulters never prosecuted, then their own deaths went unexplained. However, Rajiv was confident justice had been served in the end, even if it went against everything he believed as a policeman. He liked John; he was a good man and never deserved to have suffered as much as he did. That's why he was concerned about Surya Patil digging up the file again. What was he up to? It couldn't be good.

Rajiv drained the remains of his tea and looked around for a rubbish bin. Not finding one, he shrugged and tossed the cup onto the growing pile of discarded cups beside the bicycle.

"Constable," he called out and opened the door to the SUV. Climbing in, he waited for his driver to return and start the engine.

He didn't have a phone number for John, in fact, he had no idea where he was living these days but might have an email address for him somewhere. He would check as soon as he was back in the office.

The driver looked over at Rajiv, a question on his face.

"The station."

6

"Hello."

"Mr. Patil? This is Steve Jones. You asked me to give you a daily report."

"Yes."

"Good morning."

"Good morning."

Steve decided not to waste any more time on pleasantries. Surya Patil's tone was abrupt and matter of fact.

"Mr. Patil, the couple spent the morning at the Dubai Mall, mainly window shopping. They didn't appear to buy much. They stopped for coffee at a café late morning before returning to the hotel by Uber. They ordered room service for lunch, then didn't leave the room until the evening. At seven p.m., they had a couple of drinks at the hotel bar, then left in an Uber. I followed them to the Burj Khalifa, where they dined at the Italian Restaurant in the Armani Hotel. They were there for two-and-a-half hours before returning to your hotel at eleven pm."

"Did they meet anyone?"

"No, they were alone together the whole time."

There was a grunt of acknowledgment.

"Mr. Patil, do you still want me to follow them?"

"Of course. You keep following them until I say stop, do you understand me?"

"I understand." Steve smiled. He was happy to continue for as long as Patil was paying him. He glanced at the lifts as the doors opened onto the lobby, tensing as he watched John and Adriana walk out, followed by a bellhop with their bags.

"Ah, Mr. Patil, I have to go, it looks like they're checking out." Steve heard what sounded like a curse in another language.

"Follow them. Don't lose them! I want to know where they're going!"

"I'm on it." Steve ended the call and sank back into the sofa, making himself look as inconspicuous as he could as John and Adriana approached the front desk. Shit! Where were they going?

7

Steve waited until John and Adriana completed checking out, then watched them walk across to the hotel exit. A black Mercedes S Class with the hotel logo on the door pulled up outside, and the lid of the trunk popped up. Steve stood, slung his messenger bag over his shoulder, and walked casually toward the exit. The bellhop loaded the suitcases into the trunk, then Steve watched John hand over a tip to the bellhop before joining Adriana inside the car. The car pulled out of the porte-cochere and Steve sprinted for the door. Odds were, they were headed for the airport, but he couldn't take a chance and lose them. The lobby doors sliding open as he approached, he ran outside, his arm in the air, already signaling for a taxi. A taxi parked in the hotel driveway flashed its lights and moved toward him. Steve turned and kept his eyes on the Mercedes as it pulled out onto the main road and joined the traffic flow.

"Come on, come on," he muttered, and as soon as the taxi reached him, he yanked open the door and jumped in. "Follow that Mercedes," he pointed at the car disappearing up the road. *"Yalla, Yalla.* Hurry!"

The driver's eyes flicked to the rearview mirror, and he grunted before pulling out.

Steve leaned forward in his seat, straining his eyes to keep sight of the Mercedes ahead. The traffic flowed smoothly as they left The Palm at Jumeirah, the Mercedes still far in front, but they caught up as the traffic slowed and bunched before joining Sheikh Zayed Road. Steve instructed the driver to keep pace with the Mercedes about three cars behind as they followed the expressway into the city. After twenty minutes, they crossed the Dubai Creek, and the Mercedes indicated and left the expressway at the Casablanca Street exit. Steve thought fast. He was relieved he always carried his passport in his bag. It looked more and more likely they were heading for the airport, and if he needed to follow them onto the plane, he could.

Where Casablanca Street joined Airport Road, the Mercedes indicated right and after a couple of minutes, pulled up outside the airport terminal. Steve thrust a handful of *dirhams* at the driver and climbed out as soon as he pulled to a stop. Dashing into the terminal, he took up position next to a magazine kiosk where he could observe them through the glass without being spotted.

Steve waited until they entered the terminal, then followed them toward the check-in counter for Oman Air. Steve breathed a sigh of relief. As a Dubai resident, he wouldn't need a visa. Pulling out his phone, he dialed Surya Patil's number.

"Yes," came the gruff reply Steve expected.

"Mr. Patil, it's Steve Jones..."

"I know who it is. Where are they going?"

Steve took a deep breath. "Mr. Patil, they are checking in for the 12:25 flight to Muscat. What do you want me to do?"

"Follow them."

Steve paused, watching John and Adriana collect their boarding passes and turn away from the check-in counter.

"Are you sure? Last minute tickets will be expensive."

"I told you to follow them. Call me from Muscat."

Steve was about to confirm when he realized he was listening to a dial tone. He shrugged. Well, if Surya Patil was paying, who was he to question him? Whatever this John Hayes had done, he had made a big enemy in Surya Patil.

·

8

The flight from Dubai to Muscat was short, taking just over an hour. Steve used the time to grab a quick nap, something he'd learned in his last three years as a private eye—grab sleep whenever he could.

The seatbelt light chimed off as the plane reached the terminal and less than half the passengers stood up to deplane. The remaining passengers, Filipinos, Indians, and young Eastern-European women stayed onboard for the immediate return flight to Dubai. Steve had taken one of these flights before and learned most of the passengers were doing visa runs, leaving Dubai for the exit stamp so they could re-enter and renew their visas, Muscat the closest and cheapest destination for them. Steve stayed in his seat as John and Adriana removed their carry-on from the overhead bin at the front of the cabin, then he too stood and joined the deplaning passengers.

Immigration was a mere formality, the smiling immigration officer welcoming him to Oman. Steve bypassed the luggage belts and exited directly into the arrivals hall, waiting for John and Adriana to come through with their luggage. Steve scanned the waiting crowd for a sign with John Hayes' name on it but couldn't spot one, so he assumed they would hire a vehicle. He wandered over to the rental car kiosks and sat down on a chair, pretending to study his phone. Sure enough, ten minutes later, John and Adriana arrived to pick up a car.

Fifteen minutes later, Steve sat in a taxi following their white Toyota Land Cruiser out of the airport and onto Sultan Qaboos Street, heading east into Muscat. Traffic was thick, but Steve had no trouble keeping the Land Cruiser in sight, the red number plates of the hire car distinguishing it from all the other white Land Cruisers on the road.

After ten minutes, the Land Cruiser slowed and took the Al Khuwayr exit. Near the Japanese Embassy, they turned right into Al Saruj Street, then left toward the beach before turning into the entrance for the Grand Hyatt. Steve grinned. The job was looking better and better—nothing like an all-expenses-paid stay in a luxury hotel. He hoped Surya Patil stuck to his word and covered all his expenses. Steve stopped the taxi on the road, paid the driver, and stepped out onto the footpath. After the chilled interior of the taxi, the heat outside took his breath away. The sooner he got inside, the better.

He approached the hotel and saw John and Adriana had already entered, so he followed them in and spotted them at the check-in desk. Walking over to a waiting area, he sat down, picking up a magazine and opening it before studying John and Adriana over the top of the magazine. He didn't have contacts here in Muscat, but he needed to find out which room they were in. John and Adriana headed toward the lift, room key in hand, and Steve listened as the receptionist called out to the bellboy, "*Ithnay eashar sifr ithnan.*"

Steve grinned. He didn't speak much Arabic, but he knew his numbers—twelve zero two. Time for him to get himself a room and a car.

9

Surya Patil ended the call and threw the phone onto the sofa beside him.

"Shit." He clenched his fist and banged it on his thigh. Oman. The bastard had murdered his son and was now swanning around the world, having a great time. That wasn't right. He removed his wallet from his pocket and opened it, looking at the photo in the clear plastic sleeve. Tears welled up in his eyes, and the flesh around his chin trembled.

"Sunil, *nanna maga*." He sniffed and wiped his nose with his spare hand. With his other hand, he touched the photo. "My son." He closed the wallet, put it back in his pocket, and stood up. Walking over to the mini-bar, he pulled the cap off the bottle of whiskey and poured a large measure into a glass, knocking it back in one go, then refilled it. Carrying the glass over to the window, he stared out across the sea.

Somehow, he had to avenge his son's death. He couldn't live with himself, knowing he had found his son's killer and done nothing about it. But how? He needed to find a way. Dubai would have been difficult but not impossible. There were enough members of the Indian underworld who called Dubai home, he would have found someone to do it for him eventually. But now they were in Oman, it would be much more difficult. The most important thing was he didn't lose him, but this Australian guy seemed to be doing a good job. Surya would have preferred to use a fellow Indian —the shared culture, and his status as a senior Indian politician giving him more control—but the Australian had come highly recommended, recommended by a friend who caught his wife having an affair on one of her increasingly frequent 'shopping' jaunts to Dubai.

He looked down at the glass, swirling the whiskey around against the sides. The expenses were creeping up, and he would need to transfer more money, but he would stick with Steve until he came up with a plan to get his son the justice he deserved.

He raised the glass and drained it in one go. He would work it out. He was Surya Patil.

10

John gasped, the hair on his arms standing up. He didn't believe in God and rarely visited places of worship, but this building was spectacular.

"It's stunning."

Adriana said nothing, and he looked over at her. She stood, her neck tipped back, her mouth open, her eyes filled with tears. He was about to hug her, then remembered where he was and settled for squeezing her arm before going back to looking around the Mosque.

The Sultan Qaboos Grand Mosque was their first stop of the day. The rest of the day would have to be spectacular to outdo this. Spread out before him, in an intricate Persian design of greens, reds, and creams, was the second largest handmade single piece carpet in the world. It covered the entire forty-six thousand square feet of the prayer hall. Towering three hundred feet above them was the main dome, ornately decorated in green and gold floral patterns. The scale was breathtaking. John looked down at the guidebook in his hand.

"It says here, this is one of the largest chandeliers in the world. It weighs eight and a half tons and contains over six hundred thousand Swarovski crystals."

"It's beautiful."

"Are you glad we came?" John smiled.

She smiled back, reached over and took his hand, giving it a squeeze before letting go.

"Very happy."

"Come, let's look at the gardens before it gets too hot."

They wound their way through the groups of selfie-taking tourists, headed outside onto the glistening marble of the inner courtyard, and from there, into the formal gardens. The air was thick with the sweet fragrance from acres of freshly watered orange and yellow marigolds. Mynahs squawked and screeched from the Asoka Trees and Frangipanis bordering the garden while far overhead, a jet smudged a vapor trail across the deep blue sky.

"Stay there, my Arabian Princess," John said, pulling out his phone. He shifted slightly to ensure the minaret was correctly positioned in the background and took a photo. Adriana chuckled and adjusted her headscarf self-consciously.

"Do I still need to wear this outside?"

"I don't think so, *habibi*," John winked. "But it suits you."

Adriana laughed. "I can see why they wear it in the sun like this. It would be unbearable without something to cover your head."

"Come, let's move on." John slipped the phone into his pocket and placed his hand on the small of her back. "We should see as much as we can before it gets too hot."

They walked back toward the carpark and the parked Land Cruiser. John searched his pocket for the key fob, pressed a button, and watched the lights flash on and off as it unlocked. As he opened the door, he glanced around the carpark, now slowly filling as tour buses arrived carrying hordes of sightseeing passengers. There were a couple of other rental cars, Land Cruisers like his and the occasional saloon car. A white Pajero at the end of the carpark caught his eye... not because of the car, Pajeros almost as common as Land Cruisers on the roads of Oman, but because he thought the driver was staring at him. He looked again, but the driver, a white male, was looking down, not paying him any attention. John shrugged and slid into the driver's seat. The guy was probably checking out Adriana, and he couldn't blame him. She looked beautiful, her cream linen pants highlighting her long legs and slim hips, and her loose-fitting white cotton shirt accentuating her tan. He leaned over and kissed her on the cheek.

"*Yalla, habibi.*" He started the engine as Adriana giggled.

11

Steve slipped lower in the front seat of the Pajero and watched Adriana and John walk out the front door to their waiting Land Cruiser. They had already loaded their bags in the back, suggesting they were heading out of town. Steve cursed, realizing he had left the new clothes and toiletries he had bought earlier in his room and wouldn't be able to retrieve them. He had expected them to spend another day sightseeing in Muscat, not checking out of the hotel. Pulling out his phone, he dialed the hotel, telling them he had left early, didn't have time to check out, and to please charge the card they had on file. He would have to buy more clothes later but was grateful he had brought his bag with his passport and cash with him.

The Land Cruiser pulled out, and he started the engine, slowly pulling out after them.

He'd spent the previous day trailing them around the sights of Muscat—The Grand Mosque, The Opera House, the Souq at Muttrah, the Sultan's Al Alam Palace, and the old town with its museums and galleries. All fairly straightforward and nothing at all to give any clue why Surya Patil was so obsessed with them. They were a good-looking couple and looked very much in love with no attempt to hide it, unlike the cheating couples he followed in Dubai. They were polite and friendly to everyone they encountered and exhibited no signs of suspicious behavior. They seemed like the perfect couple.

He had phoned through his report the evening before to Surya Patil, who instructed him to keep following them. Steve didn't mind. The beautiful scenery and friendly welcoming people of Oman were a pleasant change to the fast-moving cut-throat world of Dubai. He was enjoying the change of pace, even if it did mean a lot of time sitting in the car. Another week of work like this and he would have earned enough to pay off his backlog of alimony payments and be in credit. He took a sip of coffee from the travel mug and placed it back in the cup holder before changing lanes to keep the Land Cruiser in sight as it headed east toward Qurm before turning south toward Ruwi.

After Ruwi, Steve followed them south along Route 17 as the highway wound its way inland across the Al Hajar Mountains. The landscape was barren and stark, no vegetation to be seen against the jagged brown and grey of the mountains which reached up sharp and pointed into the clear blue sky, like the incisors of a giant carnivore. Traffic was light, and Steve set the cruise control of the Pajero to just below the speed limit and settled back in his seat, the Land Cruiser just in sight ahead of him.

An hour later, the road turned east for a while before again heading south, running parallel with the coastline, and before long, the Land Cruiser indicated and exited the freeway. Steve followed, glancing at the road sign, "Bimmah Sinkhole."

The road narrowed and followed the coast through sand

and scrub, beautiful golden beaches leading to turquoise water on the left, the mountains towering high above them on the right. The Land Cruiser slowed and turned right onto a narrower road before turning left into the carpark for the Sinkhole.

Steve cruised past, deciding it was safer not to park in the same car park. He drove up the road a little way before taking a U-turn and pulling to the side where he could keep an eye on the carpark exit in the distance. There was no point in following them inside.

Reaching for his travel mug, he sipped on the remnants of his coffee, hoping he wouldn't have to wait long. He had no water, and the temperature outside was climbing, the thermometer on the dashboard showing thirty-two degrees Celsius, and it wasn't yet mid-morning.

The day continued with more of the same as John and Adriana headed further south. A visit to Wadi Shab and lunch in a resort followed the visit to Bimmah Sinkhole, then a slow drive south to the ancient seaport of Sur. Steve was tired, dehydrated, irritable, and keen to get out of the car. In Sur, while John and Adriana wandered around the shipyard, looking at the wooden dhows being constructed by hand, he loaded up on drinking water and biscuits, but there was nowhere close by to buy fresh clothing, and he was reeking of stale sweat.

From Sur, they headed south for an hour and reached the Ras al Jinz Turtle Reserve just as the sun disappeared below the horizon. Steve pulled into the parking behind them and waited, giving them enough time to check-in before he himself entered the lobby. He needed a shower, a decent meal, and then he would phone through his report to Surya Patil.

12

Surya Patil swirled the whiskey around in the glass, listening to the clink of the ice cubes against the side, then knocked back the contents in one swallow. He stood, swayed, then walked unsteadily to the bar counter in his suite and poured himself another. The private investigator was doing a good job, keeping tabs on the English dog and his girlfriend, but it was time Surya took things to the next level. What was the point in following his son's killer on his jaunts around the Middle East while Surya was stuck in a hotel suite in Dubai? He had to bring things to a close.

He removed a folded slip of paper from his pocket, squinted his eyes, and peered at the phone number scrawled on it. Nikhil Yadav had passed on the number. The number for a man who provided solutions. The man had helped Yadav—at the time Roads Minister for the Indian state of Uttar Pradesh—when a state government whistleblower, threatening to expose the corruption in road contracting bids, had fled the country and holed up in Dubai. Unfortunately for the whistleblower, he had drunk too much one night and fell to his death from his hotel balcony. Nikhil Yadav was very pleased with the result and recommended Surya give the man's service a try.

Surya took another sip of his drink, then set the glass down. He'd made tough decisions before. He hadn't gotten where he was today without removing obstacles from his path, but it had been a while since he needed to do anything drastic, preferring the use of economic pressure and influence to get things done. The days of permanently removing his rivals were in the past, but... He pulled out his wallet and looked at the picture of his son again. No-one could harm his family; he couldn't stand by and allow the killer of his son to roam free. He put the wallet down and picked up his phone. Time to make the call.

13

Bogdan Kolisnick looked down at the man sitting before him. He had made no effort to stand or even offer him a seat, remaining seated in his armchair, a glass of whiskey in his hand. He was overweight and appeared to be in his late fifties, perhaps early sixties. Despite the excess flesh, his face had a hardness, his jaw set at an arrogant angle—a man used to getting what he wanted.

Bogdan had scanned the suite as he entered. The man had money—the hotel was expensive, and the suite was one of the larger ones.

"You solved a problem for an associate of mine last year. I need a similar solution."

Bogdan nodded slowly. "Who was your associate?"

"Mr. Yadav."

Bogdan thought back over his client's names and remembered. Frowning, he looked around the room. He needed to be careful.

"That kind of solution will be expensive."

"Yadav told me." The man took a sip of his whiskey, then

gestured to an envelope lying on the coffee table. "All the information is in that envelope, together with an advance payment. I will pay the rest on a successful... ah... solution."

Bogdan nodded. Leaning over, he picked up the bulky A4-sized manila envelope. Thumbing open the flap, he looked inside. Besides a large bundle of cash, there was a single sheet of paper. He slipped it out and glanced over at the man before examining it. It was a computer printout of a photograph—a photograph of an attractive looking couple walking through a hotel lobby. It looked like the lobby downstairs. He looked up.

"Which one."

"The man."

Bogdan examined the photo again, playing close attention to the man. He looked like an average tourist—lean, not muscled, no sign of tattoos, nothing to suggest criminal links. Shouldn't be too difficult.

"Okay. When?"

"As soon as possible."

Bogdan made a face. He didn't like these rush jobs, always preferring time to prepare. Still, he would charge accordingly.

"I need more details."

14
———

Fifteen minutes later, Bogdan stepped out of the lobby and walked across to the waiting Land Cruiser idling at the curb. He climbed in and glanced across at the passenger reclining in the seat next to him, his arm shading his eyes from the light.

"We got the job."

"*Bon.* Good." The passenger sat up and raised the seatback as Bogdan reached for a crumpled pack of Marlboros on the dashboard and tapped out a cigarette. Popping out the cigarette lighter, he lit up, taking a long drag before dropping the window a couple of inches and exhaling a large cloud of smoke in the direction of the hotel lobby. His passenger waited for Bogdan to continue before giving up and prompting him.

"Well, what's the job?"

Bogdan flicked ash out the window and stared out the windscreen as if he hadn't heard. After a moment, he said, "We have to make a problem go away." He turned to his passenger. *"Pours toujours."*

"We've done that before," the passenger shrugged, his

shoulders rising as his lower lip pushed out. "As long as we get paid."

"We've got an advance," Bogdan nodded and passed over the envelope of money. "Balance on completion of the job."

Taha Kateb looked inside and raised an eyebrow. It all sounded okay, so far, so why was Bogdan so reticent? He pulled out the photograph.

"Both?"

"No, just the man."

"C'est plus facile que deux," Taha nodded. "Easier than two."

"Oui." Bogdan blew out another cloud of smoke. "That's not the issue. The problem is the target is in Oman, and the client wants the job done immediately."

"Ah."

Both men sat in silence, staring out the window. Taha spoke first. "We can't fly."

"Non." Bogdan shook his head. "We won't get through security with our weapons." He lowered the window and flicked his cigarette butt out onto the forecourt. Winding up the window, he turned to Taha. "Is your go-bag in the back?"

"Always."

"Good. We drive, and we leave now."

15

John waved at the waiter, a young man from India he had met during dinner the night before.

"Sir?"

"Aashish, good morning."

"Good morning, Sir." He turned to Adriana, "Good morning, Ma'am."

"Aashish, is there any chance we can get some fresh coffee?" John nodded in the direction of the breakfast buffet. "That coffee has been stewing for hours. I would prefer something fresh if it's not too much trouble."

"No problem, Sir," Aashish smiled, pinching the first two fingers and his thumb of the right hand together and bobbed his head in that distinctive Indian way, "Just give me two minutes, Sir."

"Sure, take your time," John smiled, watching as Aashish retreated to the kitchen. "It's tough for these boys. They spend years away from home, working day and night, just so they can send money back to their families."

"You have a soft heart, Mr. Hayes," Adriana smiled, her head tilted to one side.

John blushed a little and looked down at his plate. Realizing it was empty, he looked up, changing the subject.

"Did you get any good photos?"

Adriana sat forward. "Oh yes," she swiped open her phone screen, "Look at these, wasn't it amazing?"

They had risen at four-thirty that morning and after a quick wash, were dressed and waiting in the hotel lobby with all the other guests. From there, they were divided into groups and led by their guides through the darkness toward the beach. Their guide, a tall young Omani named Saeed, had stopped them at the top of the dunes and explained how the turtles traveled for thousands of miles, sometimes from as far away as Australia, just to lay their eggs on that very beach.

A whistle and a waved red light from among the dunes interrupted him, and he led them over to where a colleague was watching a large shape in the dark. Adriana tugged John's arm in breathless excitement as Saeed switched on his red-light torch, and they saw a huge turtle lying in a hole in the sand, a mound of glistening white eggs piling up in the hole behind her. They watched in awestruck silence for about twenty minutes as the turtle covered the eggs with sand, then finally exhausted, turned and made her way back down the beach before disappearing into the blue phosphorescence of the surf.

Aashish arrived with the coffee and poured cups for John and Adriana.

"Thank you, Aashish." John took a sip. "Much better, thank you."

"My pleasure, Sir," Aashish smiled shyly and retreated to the safety of the buffet.

"I still can't believe we saw that this morning." Adriana put the phone down and reached for her coffee cup. "To be so close to something like that was incredible."

John nodded and placed his cup back down on the table, reaching for Adriana's hand.

"I'm happy I saw it with you, *habibi*."

Adriana slapped his hand playfully and grinned.

"Shall we get moving? I'm excited to see what else this country has to show us."

John picked up his coffee cup again, took a couple of big sips, then stood up. He waited for Adriana to stand, then followed her out of the restaurant, waving goodbye to Aashish as he did. They walked through the lobby and turned the corner toward the lift, narrowly avoiding colliding with a western man coming the other way. He looked shocked and took a step back.

"I'm sorry," John said, and stood to one side, gesturing for the man to pass him.

"Ah, yeah, no worries," said the man in a distinctive Australian accent. "Thank you." He disappeared around the corner.

"Come, let's go and pack." John took Adriana by the arm and led her into the lift.

16

John closed the door behind him and walked down the corridor to the stairs, then jogged down one floor to the lobby. Adriana was just finishing up her shower, and John thought he would use the time to check out and do a final check of his email. The internet in the room was appalling, the signal only seeming to cover the lobby, but given they would be in the desert tonight, it would be the last chance of internet for a few days.

He cleared the bill with the receptionist, then sat down in one of the sofas in the lobby. Opposite him, an Omani man with two young children smiled at him, his wife busy shopping in the gift boutique behind them.

"Good morning."

The man nodded, then spoke to his children in Arabic. They looked up hesitantly, stood to attention, then said softly to John, "Good morning."

John grinned and gave them a thumbs up before turning his attention to his phone. He checked the weather for the Wahiba Sands area. Forty-three degrees Celsius was predicted for the middle of the day. Thank goodness the

Land Cruiser was new and had an efficient air-conditioner. He hoped the air-conditioning in the desert camp would be just as good. The temperature was forecasted to only drop ten to fifteen degrees at night, but it would still be a good experience. The desert had always fascinated John, growing up on a diet of Lawrence of Arabia and Beau Geste stories when he was a kid. He was looking forward to it. He switched to the news and skimmed through the headlines. Nothing of real note, the usual bad news, the normal posturing of political leaders—the U.S. declaring imminent victory in their war in Syria, Israel and Palestine still at each other's throats, and Saudi Arabia's proxy war in Yemen entering the sixth year—nothing changed. John wouldn't miss internet access while in the desert.

He opened his emails and scanned the subject lines and senders. Again, nothing of great interest—a couple of emails from various newsletters he followed and a bank statement for his account in Hong Kong. He skipped through them all until he saw a sender who caught his attention—Rajiv Sampath.

He leaned back in his chair and stared blankly at the window of the gift boutique. Detective Inspector Rajiv Sampath of the Indian Police Service—a name he hoped never to hear again. The memories of those dark days in Bangalore stirred and threatened to come to the surface, but John pushed them back down. What did he want after all this time? Just a friendly chat? John didn't think so. His body filled with dread, all the joy from an early morning spotting turtles, leaving his body. Shit. John stared down at the phone screen and bit his lip. He had to find out. He tapped on the email and started reading.

17

It was an uneventful drive, the road winding through the rugged sand-colored crags of the *Jebels*. Miles and miles of sand and stone, interspersed with dusty shrubs and now and then, a herd of wild camels. It was stark and bleak but beautiful.

They had backtracked to Sur before heading inland, and from Sur, the traffic had been light, Adriana dozing in the seat beside him after their early morning start. Midway, they made a toilet stop, topping up their caffeine levels at a local roadside coffee stall staffed by smiling Indians and Bangladeshis.

Adriana adjusted her sunglasses and tilted her head to one side. "Are you okay, John? You've been silent since we left the Turtle Reserve."

John toyed with the paper coffee cup on the table in front of him before looking up. He shrugged, "I'm fine."

Adriana nodded slowly. "Is there something on your mind?"

"No, no." John gave her a quick smile before looking away and staring into the distance. "Maybe a little tired."

At that moment, a black and white Dodge Charger pulled up, and two traffic police climbed out.

"Wow, I've never seen a police car like that." John jumped up, eager to change the subject. "I'm just going to have a look while you finish your coffee."

Adriana watched him walk away, sure something wasn't right. She'd caught John in dark moods before when he thought he was alone, but he shrugged them off when she was around. Most of the time, he was happy and carefree. She watched him chat with the policemen proud to show off their car. Perhaps it was to do with John's past. He had hinted at dark times and said he would tell her one day when the time was right, but she still didn't know what had happened and was reluctant to push things. Their relationship was young, and she didn't want to spoil it.

They were still processing the events in the refugee camp in Thailand. She didn't know everything that occurred but suspected John had to do things he regretted, even if it was for the greater good. Draining the rest of her coffee, she stood up. John turned to look at her and smiled, his mood already better. Perhaps she was worrying unnecessarily.

18

Refreshed after their short coffee break, they drove on to the small desert town of Bidiyah, reaching it at two-thirty in the afternoon. The town wasn't known for much more than a stopping off point before heading into the dunes of the Wahiba Sands. The desert camp had instructed them to stop at the filling station just off the highway to top up the fuel tank and reduce the air pressure in the tires, a lower tire pressure providing more traction in the sand.

John turned off the main road and pulled up beside three battered pickups. A Bedouin man, in a dirty *dishdasha* and a red and white checked *shemagh* knotted untidily around his head, climbed out of one of the pickups and tapped on John's window.

"As salaam aleikum."

"Wa aleikum salaam," John replied.

The Bedouin raised an eyebrow in surprise and peered inside at Adriana before looking back at John.

"Ah, you speak Arabic?"

"No, not at all." John had a feeling where the conversation was heading, and sure enough, the Bedouin continued.

"You will need a guide. The dunes are very tough. This morning, already a car has got stuck."

John pursed his lips and studied the man's face. He was confident their Land Cruiser would have no trouble in the sand, but he asked anyway, "How much?"

The Bedouin quoted a ridiculous price, confirming John's suspicions.

"No, thank you," he smiled politely, shook his head, and pressed the button to close the window. As the glass slid shut, the Bedouin continued in a last-ditch sales pitch.

"Sir, the conditions are very bad. The sand has hidden the tracks. It is very dangerous if you get stuck out there."

John smiled through the closing window and put the vehicle in gear. The Bedouin muttered something unpleasant in Arabic and turned to look back at the other waiting pickups. John pulled away and drove in beside the petrol pumps.

"Do you think we need a guide?" Adriana asked.

"I doubt it. These guys hope most tourists will be too scared to drive themselves. And that price seems ridiculous." John opened the door and looked back. "Anyway, I'll get a second opinion." He climbed out and smiled at the pump attendant.

"Good morning."

"Good morning, Sir."

"Full tank, please."

The attendant, a young man in filthy overalls, opened the fuel cap and inserted the nozzle. He indicated to John to check the pump meter was at zero, then pumped the gas.

John glanced toward the pickups where the drivers stood staring in his direction.

"Where are you from, my friend?" he asked the attendant.

"India."

"Which part?"

"Kerala, Sir."

"There are so many people from Kerala working in Oman."

The attendant nodded but continued staring at the fuel pump, watching the numbers on the meter tick over.

"I used to live in India," John continued, trying to strike up a rapport. "Almost two years."

The attendant glanced at him and smiled.

"It's a lovely country. It must be hard being so far from home."

"Yes, Sir." The attendant scuffed at the concrete forecourt with the toe of his boot before looking up. "But I need the work."

"Do you miss home?"

The attendant nodded just as the pump clicked off. He removed the nozzle, and John handed over a handful of *rials*.

"Keep the change."

The young man's face lit up in a big grin. "Thank you, Sir."

John opened the vehicle door, then as if as in afterthought turned back.

"Do I need a guide to take me to the desert camps?"

The attendant's eyes flicked toward the Bedouin, then he turned away, so his face was away from them.

"No, Sir. This vehicle will make it easily."

"Thank you, my friend," John smiled and patted the young man on the shoulder. "Now, where can I let the air out of the tires?"

"There is a tire shop around the corner. My friend runs it. He will help you."

John climbed back into the Land Cruiser and looked across at Adriana. "As I thought, we don't need a guide."

"Why are they trying to scare us?"

John shrugged. "Everyone has to make a living."

He pulled away from the pumps, glancing in his rearview mirror as he did so. The three Bedouin drivers had surrounded the pump attendant and judging by their hand gestures, were not happy.

John drove out of the petrol station and onto the service road running parallel with the main highway. Two buildings along, he spotted the tire shop, another Land Cruiser already in one of the bays, a mechanic crouching beside the rear tire. John pulled over, and a man rushed over, a big smile on his face.

"Hello, Sir, how are you?" He reached in through the window and grasped John's hand. "You need to let the air out?"

"Yes, how much?"

"For you, Sir, two *rials*."

John grinned, and switched to Hindi, thankful he had learned some bargaining skills while living in India. *"Yeh bahut mehnga, bhai.* That is very expensive, brother."

The man took a step back in shock, then his face broke into a big grin.

"Sir, you speak my language. I thought you were a normal tourist. For you, my friend, there is no charge."

"Shukriya," John smiled. "Thank you. What is your name?"

"Ahmed." He reached out his hand again, and John shook it firmly.

"John."

Ahmed turned and called out to a mechanic who came trotting over with a small hand tool.

"A little of the local language always helps," John grinned at Adriana.

"My hero," Adriana winked.

John climbed down and watched as the mechanic removed the valve from each tire, the air hissing out before replacing the valve and checking the pressure with the hand tool.

"It should be twenty for the sand," Ahmed explained, referring to the air pressure. "Which camp are you staying in?"

"The Scheherazade Camp. Is it good?"

"One of the best, my friend. How many nights?"

"Just the one."

"Okay, tomorrow when you come back, I will look after you and pump up the tires again."

"Do I need a guide?"

"Ha, no, it's an easy road in a four-wheel drive." He waved toward the filling station. "Don't listen to those men. They are..." he paused, searching for the word, "wolves."

John laughed as the mechanic finished all four tires and nodded at Ahmed before returning to the workshop.

Ahmed turned to John, "All done my friend. See you tomorrow."

John held out two *rials*.

"No, no..." Ahmed shook his head and pushed his hand away. "You are my friend."

"Ahmed where are you from?"

"Bangladesh."

"Your family is there?"

"Yes, my wife and my daughter."

"Then take this for them." John thrust the money back

into Ahmed's hand. "I will see you tomorrow. *Khuda hafiz.* God be with you."

Ahmed clasped John's hand in both of his. *"Allah hafiz,* my friend."

John climbed back into the Land Cruiser. "Let's go."

Ahmed waved as they drove off.

"You've made a friend there," said Adriana.

They drove past the scowling Bedouin guides, and John couldn't resist waving in their direction.

"And some enemies there."

19

After leaving the fuel station, John pulled over and checked the GPS coordinates on his phone. According to the phone map, the camp was in the middle of a vast, empty space with no roads and no settlements. John confirmed the coordinates, then from the filling station, followed the road leading toward the desert as it led through the suburbs, past modest single-story houses and mud walls. After five minutes, the tarmac ended, and he slowed as the road became hard packed sand, covered in wheel tracks leading off into the distance. John checked the GPS again to make sure he was heading in the correct direction, then drove onto the sand.

Small settlements lined each side of the track, the buildings humble and ramshackle, their compounds fenced with wire and sticks. Goats were plentiful, but there wasn't a camel in sight, the ship of the desert replaced by the Bedouin's new transport of choice, the battered Toyota pickup. Before long, they crested a rise, and the desert opened up before them, miles and miles of sand as far as the eye could see. The track they were following widened, wheel tracks spreading out to each side as vehicles had sought for traction in the ever-shifting sands. John accelerated into the open space but soon slowed as the corrugations caused by the passage of vehicles made the speed uncomfortable. They drove slowly for a while until another vehicle passed them at high speed, leaving them behind in a cloud of dust.

"How is he going so fast?" John sped up, and the vibration got worse and worse until he reached a speed where the vibration stopped, the Land Cruiser's tires skimming across the top of the corrugations. John looked down at the speedometer.

"We're doing ninety!"

The Land Cruiser slammed down into a dip, and John wrestled with the wheel to gain control as Adriana's head hit the roof.

"Shit," John braked hard, then glanced across at Adriana with a grin. "I think slower is safer."

20

The white Pajero pulled into the tire bay, and the driver climbed out.

Ahmed rushed over a big smile on his face, happy to find another tourist to prey upon.

"Good morning Sir, how are you?"

The western man smiled. "Good mate. Can you let the air out of my tires?"

"Of course, Sir, of course."

"How much.?"

"For you, Sir, only two *rials*."

"Okay."

Ahmed waved his mechanic over and stood back and watched as he let the tires down.

The tourist stood, watching with his hands on his hips, beads of sweat forming on his forehead in the afternoon sun.

The mechanic finished, and the man held out two *rials*. Ahmed took it with a smile and pocketed it.

"When you come back, I will pump the tires for you free."

"Thanks, mate." The man opened the car door and climbed in. Before closing it, he asked, "Hey, I'm trying to catch up with my friend and his wife. They are in a white Land Cruiser."

"Ah, Mr. John," Ahmed smiled. "He just left here."

"Good, I'm not too far behind."

Ahmed removed the two *rials* from his pocket. "Please take this back. No charge for Mr. John's friend."

"No, mate, you keep it. Say, how long will it take to get to the camp from here?"

"The Scheherazade Camp? Maybe one-and-a-half hours?"

The westerner grinned. "Thanks, mate."

He closed the door, and Ahmed watched him as he drove off, wondering why John didn't mention his friend following him. And why waste money on a separate hire car? He shrugged. Some of these tourists had too much money. A vehicle beeped behind him, and he turned his attention to the next four-wheel drive loaded with travelers.

21

Steve grinned as he pulled away from the tire shop. That information was easy to get. It always amazed him how trusting people were if you were confident and friendly. He indicated left, pulled out onto the main road, and followed the GPS instructions along the narrow road as it wound its way through areas of dilapidated commercial buildings and sand-colored houses behind crumbling walls. After ten minutes, the road opened up again just before the tar macadam ended and gave way to a wide sandy track with small settlements to each side. Steve slowed and pulled over to check his cell phone—only two bars. He'd better report to Mr. Patil before he lost the signal altogether. He was sure there would be no cell phone coverage once he was out in the dunes. The phone rang three times before the familiar gruff voice answered.

"Yes?"

"Mr. Patil? It's Steve Jones."

"I know."

"Ah... I've followed Mr. Hayes to a town called Bidiyah. He is staying the night in a desert camp in an area called the

Wahiba Sands. I thought I would call in now since there will be no cell phone coverage once I go into the desert."

There was no reply from the other end of the line for a while, and Steve thought the line had got cut.

"Hello?"

"How long will he be in the desert?" Surya asked.

"I don't know. I understand people usually only stay one night, though."

"Hmm, so it has to be tonight."

"I'm sorry?" Steve wasn't sure what Surya was referring to.

"Where are you now?"

"I'm parked just before entering the desert."

"Wait there."

"I'm sorry, what?" Steve frowned.

"I said, wait there. I'm sending someone to meet you."

Steve scratched his head. "Who?"

"It doesn't matter. Text me your location and car number. Someone will meet you."

Steve stared with confusion out the windscreen. "Mr. Patil, I don't understand."

"Your work is done. Thank you. Someone will meet you. When they come, give them a description of John Hayes' vehicle and tell them the location of the camp, then you can leave."

Steve narrowed his eyes. "But..."

"Send me your final bill, and I'll transfer the money immediately." The line went dead.

Steve dropped the phone onto the seat beside him and rubbed his face with both hands, letting out a long sigh.

"Oh well, it was a good earner while it lasted," he said out loud.

He glanced at the clock on the dashboard. All he could

do now was wait.

22

It was three hours later when Steve saw a dusty, white Toyota Land Cruiser appear in the rearview mirror, flash its lights, then pull in behind him. Two men sat inside. Steve sat up, stretched his neck from side-to-side, and opened the door.

"About time," he muttered as he stepped out. The time had dragged, and he had dozed off, only waking up to pee and turn the engine on and off, intermittently cooling the interior with the airconditioning.

He walked toward the car and studied the two men as he approached. Neither made any attempt to get out of the vehicle, just watched him approach through dark sunglasses.

The driver's window slid down as he neared, and Steve looked inside. The driver appeared to be Caucasian, his face unsmiling, hair cropped short but two days growth of beard on his chin. His passenger looked to be of Middle Eastern origin, olive skin, stubble also covering his cheeks. Both were dressed in loose, sand-colored cotton shirts and cargo pants. Neither made any attempt to speak.

Steve cleared his throat. "Did Mr. Patil send you?"

The driver nodded.

Steve put his hand out, "Steve Jones."

The driver shook his hand, his grip firm, his hand hard and calloused. His sleeve slipped up to reveal a tattooed forearm.

"Where is the camp?" The driver spoke with an accent Steve couldn't place. European? Perhaps Eastern Europe?

"The Scheherazade Camp." Steve gestured toward the track leading into the desert. "About an hour and a half that way. I believe it's signposted."

"Good. We'll find it."

The passenger spoke for the first time. "What's he driving?"

Steve's first impression was correct, his accent distinctly Arabic.

"A white Toyota Land Cruiser like this one. Red plates, number 7359."

The passenger nodded but said nothing more.

"We'll take it from here," said the driver.

"What are you planning to do?"

The driver studied Steve for a moment, his forehead creasing in a frown.

"That's between Mr. Patil and us. Thank you for your help." The window slid closed, putting an end to the conversation.

The Land Cruiser moved forward, and as it passed, Steve glanced into the back, trying to get an idea of their intentions, but the glare of the sun on the window prevented him from seeing anything other than a couple of bags, and by then, the vehicle had moved past. He glanced at the number plates and frowned—a Dubai registration. They had come a long way.

Steve shrugged. None of his business. He had done his bit. Time to head home.

23

Steve climbed into his Pajero, glanced in the mirror, then turned the vehicle around in a U-turn, heading back into town. If he hurried, he could be back in Muscat by night and catch the last flight back to Dubai.

He pulled up outside a small grocery store, turned off the engine, and went inside. He was thirsty, the time spent sitting waiting for the two men dehydrating him, and he was hungry.

A group of young Omani boys crowded the counter, buying sweets and soft drinks. While Steve waited to pay, he thought over the events of the last few days. It had been a good job. By the time he submitted his final bill, he would have earned enough to clear his outstanding debts and have some cash left over until the next job came up. Hopefully, Mr. Patil would recommend him to other clients.

The boys finished their purchases and noisily exited the shop, chattering and pushing and shoving each other. Steve stepped forward and placed the bottles of water and a packet of biscuits on the counter, nodding at the elderly shopkeeper.

There was something about those guys in the car that seemed off though. Steve had spent many years as a country policeman in rural Australia, and although crime had been low, he had still developed a sixth sense for when things weren't right.

After the shopkeeper handed back the change, Steve scooped up his purchases and headed back to the car. Sitting inside, he dumped them on the seat beside him, started the engine, turned the air-conditioning on full, and opened a bottle of water. He drank half before pulling out onto the road and heading toward the highway.

He wondered what the issue was between John Hayes and Surya Patil. In all his observations of John and the woman accompanying him, he'd seen them be nothing but nice to everyone they dealt with. In fact, Surya Patil seemed the more doubtful of them all. Steve shrugged. He indicated and turned onto Route 23, heading north toward Muscat.

Steve drummed his fingers on the steering wheel. The two men were definitely sketchy, something about their energy. Steve sighed. Maybe he was paranoid. It was his job just to follow and report back. He had done that. Now, his responsibilities were over—time to head back to Dubai and put his feet up for a while.

He glanced up at the road signs hanging over the highway—two hundred kilometers to Muscat. If he stuck to the speed limit, he would easily be at the airport within three hours. A sign flashed for an exit a kilometer ahead. Steve gripped the steering wheel and bit his bottom lip.

"Bugger!" he indicated and pulled over onto the hard shoulder. He picked up the bottle of water and drained the contents as he sat, staring at the exit sign. Something wasn't right, of that he was sure, but why should he get involved? It was nothing more to do with him. Steve did a quick mental calculation of the outstanding fees he was owed by Mr. Patil, and made his decision. What went on in other people's lives was none of his business. He had done his job and was paid well for it. Time to move on. He looked in his mirror, then pulled out on to the highway. Time to head back to Dubai.

24

After about forty-five minutes, the long wide desert valley ended in a wall of dunes, and a battered tin sign pointed to a track leading up the side of a dune towering above them.

John slowed for the turn and cautiously climbed the track. The sand was much deeper, and he had to twist the steering wheel side-to-side at times to find traction. However, the powerful V6 engine always pulled the Land Cruiser out of difficulty. The track switched back on itself a couple of times as they gained height until finally, they crested the dune. Before them, spreading as far as the horizon, was a sea of sand, the dunes folding into each other like waves in the ocean.

"Wow!" Adriana exclaimed. "It's stunning."

John pulled to a stop, wound down the windows, and turned off the engine. Reaching across, he rested his hand on Adriana's thigh. She placed her hand on top of his and gave it a squeeze as they gazed at the view—not a building, tree, animal, or human being in any direction. It was breathtaking in its scale and beauty... and silent. Completely silent, the only sound coming from the ticking of the cooling engine.

"I can't believe how big it is," Adriana broke the silence. "Sand everywhere."

"It's over twelve thousand square kilometers." John pointed toward what he guessed was South. "If you keep driving that way, you'll eventually reach the coast." He pointed West. "Way over that way is Saudi Arabia."

"Incredible," Adriana sighed. "Does anyone live here? Is it possible?"

"From what I've read, the Bedouin used to, but..." John shrugged. "I think now they've moved to the cities and settlements like the one we drove through at the beginning. I think the notion of crisscrossing the sands in caravans of camels doesn't exist anymore. They all seem to be driving Toyotas."

With the windows down and the air-conditioning off, the heat inside the vehicle quickly became uncomfortable, and John glanced across at Adriana,

"Should we go?"

"Yes," Adriana nodded.

John started the engine, wound up the windows, and selected Drive. The car moved a little, but the tires spun and bogged down in the soft sand.

"Damn."

"What's the matter?"

"We're stuck."

John shifted into Park, selected low ratio, then attempted to drive off again. The wheels spun, throwing rooster tails of sand behind them. He twisted the steering wheel side-to-side, pumping the accelerator. The wheels continued spinning, the vehicle shifting forward slowly at first, then picking up speed as they found traction on a harder packed section of sand. John chuckled nervously as they continued along the track.

"Phew! I think we need to be careful where we stop in the future. I wouldn't want to get stuck out here."

"Were you worried?" Adriana asked.

John glanced across at her and grinned, "A little bit." He switched his attention back to the route, avoiding the deeper sand. "I don't think it would be too bad, though. Judging by the wheel tracks, I think a lot of vehicles pass this way. Someone would come along and help us."

"Looking at the amount of garbage strewn by the side of the track, I think you're right."

"Yeah," John sighed. "It's horrible what we're doing to the planet. A beautiful place like this and people can't take their garbage with them."

They drove on for another thirty minutes until John squinted when he saw something in the distance. Removing his sunglasses, he peered forward.

"Look, I think that's our camp ahead."

Fifteen minutes later, he pulled onto a smooth-packed area of sand where a row of four-wheel drives was already parked. John switched off the engine, and they climbed out of the vehicle. To the side of the parking, a wire-fenced enclosure held a small herd of Arabian Oryx and three camels. In front, one of the only two permanent-looking structures housed the reception area while further away to the left, a sand-colored, two-story building housed what looked to be the dining area, kitchen, and staff quarters. From the reception, the land sloped down and away toward a cluster of large black and white Bedouin-style tents.

"We are staying in those?" Adriana exclaimed.

"Yes, *habibi*."

She clapped her hands together. "Let's go! This will be fun."

25

Their accommodation looked unremarkable from the outside, a large rectangular shaped tent, made from black cloth with white stripes running horizontally around the sides. Adriana walked closer and felt the cloth.

"What's it made of?"

"Wool, ma'am," said the camp staff member carrying their bags. "The Bedouin weave it from goat and sheep wool."

"But it's black, doesn't it get hot?" Adriana asked, a puzzled expression on her face.

"Please, see inside," the boy smiled and opened the tent door, standing aside to allow them to walk in.

"Wow."

Although appearing to be a traditional Bedouin tent on the outside, inside, it was like a luxury hotel room. A large bedroom with a king-sized bed and a small sitting area took up most of the space, and through a door to the rear of the tent was a spacious bathroom suite, the roof open to the sky.

Persian rugs covered the floor of the tent, and the interior was chilled by an efficient portable air-conditioning unit running off a central generator behind the dining area.

"Ma'am, Sir, it's cool now because we have the air-conditioning, but traditionally, the tents would be much cooler than outside, anyway. I don't know why, but it just seems to work."

"Yes, I've read about this," said John, turning to Adriana. "Apparently, the sun heats the black cloth which causes hot air to rise, and that draws out air from inside, creating a cooling breeze. It's brilliant, actually." John waved toward the air-conditioning unit and grinned. "Of course, this is much better for us. I think cooler is a relative term for the Bedouin."

The boy arranged their bags, then asked, "Will there be anything else, Sir?"

"No, thank you." John reached into his pocket and removed some *rials* and passed them over. "What's your name?"

"Fouad, Sir."

"Thank you, Fouad. What time is the sunset?"

"Sir, around six-thirty, Sir. If you want to see it, I recommend you climb the big dune behind the camp. You can get a wonderful view from up there. You should leave at six. It will be cooler then and give you enough time to climb up."

"Thank you, Fouad. *Shukraan.*"

Fouad grinned. "*Afwan.* You are welcome." He bowed his head and retreated from the tent, pulling the tent door closed as he did.

John looked at his watch, then grinned. "We still have a couple of hours, *habibi.*" He took Adriana's hand and led her toward the bed. "No sense in wasting time."

Just before sunset, they climbed barefoot up the high dunes above the camp and sat in the cool sand, waiting for the sun to go down. Tracks of small rodents and birds crisscrossed the sand around them, but otherwise, there was no sign of life. The sun sank lower in the sky, the sand changing from gold to pink as the sky turned from blue to black. Adriana leaned against John, his arm around her. As the sun disappeared below the horizon in a bright red flaming ball, the sky filled with a vast display of twinkling stars.

"Isn't it beautiful?" Adriana murmured, then turned her head and planted a kiss on John's cheek. "Thank you."

John smiled and squeezed her tighter, at last happy he had someone in his life to share moments like this.

Glancing at his watch, he said, "Come let's make our way back to camp before we lose all the light. I'm starving." They rose, and holding Adriana's hand, he led her down the steep face of the dune as she giggled and stumbled in the sand. At the bottom, they retrieved their shoes and dusted the sand from their legs and feet before heading toward the dining area.

Kerosene lamps on poles lit the path, and from the dining area, the flickering light from a bonfire cast moving shadows across the sand. In front of the tents, a Bedouin woman sat on a carpet spread on the sand, a selection of handcrafts spread out before her.

"*As salaam aleikum,*" she called out, "please look."

Adriana squatted down beside her and examined the goods—hand-knotted bracelets made from goat's wool in many colors, key rings, and talismans. John studied the woman as she joked and chatted with Adriana. Clad in the traditional all covering *abaya* of the Bedouin, her head was covered by a headscarf. A polished silver mask covered her nose and mouth, protecting her from the sun and the sand. It looked severe, but her eyes twinkled with mischief. John tuned in to her conversation.

"You are from?" she asked Adriana.

"Portugal," Adriana smiled.

The woman jerked her head toward John, "Husband?"

Adriana smiled and shook her head.

"Boyfriend?" the woman asked with a cackle.

Adriana chuckled too and looked up at John. John winked but said nothing.

Changing the subject, Adriana asked, "What is your name?"

"My name is Warda," she said, pronouncing the w like a v. "You?"

"Adriana."

"A-dr-i-aa-na." Warda repeated. "Adriana."

"Yes. These are your daughters?" Adriana pointed at two little girls playing in the sand.

"Yes," Warda smiled. "Farida and Saara."

At the sound of their names, the girls stopped what they were doing and looked up, then feeling the eyes of John and Adriana on them, giggled and ran off behind the tents.

"Pretty girls," said Adriana. "You are very lucky."

"*Shukraan.* Thank you."

A tall man in a grey *dishdasha* approached, a multicolored *shemagh* tied messily around his head, a *Khanjar*, the large curved knife the Omani's traditionally carried, tucked into the sash around his waist. Warda pointed at him.

"My husband."

Her husband, a handsome man with a long, fine nose and a neatly trimmed goatee, nodded at Adriana, then greeted John.

"As salaam aleikum."

John held out his hand and returned the greeting.

"Wa aleikum salaam. My name is John."

"Mansur." He shook John's hand, his grip firm, his palms and fingers calloused from hard physical work. "Welcome to Scheherazade."

"Thank you."

"Your first time in the desert?"

"Yes, for both of us." John gestured toward Adriana, who rose to her feet. "It's beautiful here."

"Do you have any plans tomorrow morning?"

"No," John replied. "We thought perhaps we might get up early for the sunrise."

Mansur nodded thoughtfully, glanced at Adriana, then addressed John.

"There is a beautiful place a few kilometers from here. It's my favorite place to see the sunrise. If you like, I can take you there? You have a four-wheel drive?"

"Yes." John looked at Adriana. "What do you think?"

"I would love to."

John turned back to Mansur. "Sure. If you don't mind."

"It would be my honor. Sunrise is just before six. Can you meet me in the carpark at five?"

John looked at Adriana, who nodded.

"Yes, of course."

"Good. Please wear some warm clothes, it will be cool at that time."

John smiled at Mansur, then down at his wife. "Thank you."

Adriana squatted down again and placed her hand on Warda's.

"Thank you. I will buy something tomorrow. I left my purse in the tent."

Warda grabbed Adriana's hand in both of her own.

"It's okay, *habibi*." She leaned forward and whispered, a mischievous look on her face. "Your boyfriend is very handsome." The two of them burst into laughter.

26

Still chuckling, Adriana hooked her arm through John's as they walked the short distance to the dining area.

"Wow," said Adriana and gave John's arm a squeeze.

A large, three-sided tent faced a bonfire burning in the sand. Persian rugs covered the floor, and large multicolored cushions were arranged in communal seating on the rugs. In front of the cushions, several low wooden tables were laid with silver plates and cutlery. The darkness beyond the campfire was broken only by the kerosene lamps on poles, the lights floating in the blackness like low flying stars.

From the sand-colored brick kitchen building, the only other permanent structure in the camp, a young Omani man in a crisp white *dishdasha* emerged, an embroidered woolen *mussar* tied neatly around his head. He bowed slightly.

"Good evening, Sir, Madam. Welcome to Camp Scheherazade."

John and Adriana smiled. "Good evening."

"My name is Umar. Please make yourself comfortable,"

he said, waving toward the cushioned seating area. "Dinner will be served shortly."

John led Adriana over to the cushions and smiled at an overweight middle-aged couple already reclining on the rugs, the man taking a puff from an ornate *sheesha* pipe standing beside him.

"Good evening," John said with a nod and a smile.

"Hello," the lady smiled while the man blew a big puff of smoke into the air and nodded.

John guided Adriana to the far side of the seating area, softly explaining he preferred to be away from the smoke. They arranged the cushions, then sat down as another couple arrived. They were elderly and immaculately dressed, the man slim and straight despite his advanced years. He smiled a greeting to both couples, then helped his wife to sit down, supporting her by the arm as she lowered herself to the floor. He smiled at John.

"Good evening." His accent was distinctly German. "It's very comfortable once you are down, but at our age, it's not so easy to get there."

His wife smiled shyly as she settled into the cushions. Her husband knelt on one knee, then placed his hands on the floor and lowered himself beside her. They spoke briefly in German before the man turned to John and Adriana.

"My name is Gunther. My wife, Johanna."

John leaned forward and offered his hand. "I'm John, this is Adriana."

He shook John's hand and smiled at Adriana, who smiled back and said, "*Guten abend*."

"Ah, you speak German?"

"*Nein, ein bisschen*. Only a little."

Gunther frowned, "Your accent, *Español*?"

"No, I'm from Portugal."

"Ah yes, a beautiful country. We visit the Algarve often. We are from Germany, but I'm sorry,"—he smiled at his wife—"my wife doesn't speak English."

Johanna smiled, realizing her husband was speaking about her as Umar and one of the Indian staff appeared, placing a platter of *mezze* in front of each couple.

"Would you like something to drink?" Umar asked.

"I would like a glass of white wine," replied Gunther, "and my wife as well."

"I'm sorry, Sir, there is no alcohol here," Umar replied, making a sorry face, his hands clasped in front of his *Khanjar*.

"Ah yes, of course. How silly of me. Some sparkling water, please."

"Certainly." Umar turned to John and Adriana, "Sir, Madam?"

John looked at Adriana, "We'll have the same?"

Adriana nodded.

John leaned forward, passed a plate to Adriana, and they helped themselves to the food on the table.

"How long are you in Oman, Gunther?"

"Just ten days. It's our second time here." He paused as the Indian waiter opened a bottle of sparkling water and filled their glasses. "It is a beautiful country, and the people are friendly."

John nodded, his mouth full. He swallowed, then took a sip of water.

"It's our first time here, and we like it."

"How long are you here for?"

"We haven't decided yet," John grinned. "We're fortunate we don't have a fixed schedule."

"Yes," Gunther nodded. "It's good to travel like that. I am retired, so we also often travel without a schedule." He raised an eyebrow. "But John, I am curious, you are too young to be retired. If you don't mind me asking, what do you do for a living?"

John tore off a piece of flatbread, scooped up some hummus, and popped it into his mouth to avoid replying. What did he do? What was the best way to explain it without going into detail? He glanced over at Adriana, who was also waiting for his reply. He swallowed and took another sip of water.

"I've been lucky with investments, so I'm semi-retired."

Gunther nodded as he chewed his food. "You are fortunate, John, but if I can give you a piece of advice? As an old man who has been through this? Always keep yourself active. The idea of retirement is good, but you need to keep yourself busy. To keep the mind and body working."

"Yes," John nodded. "I agree." He winked at Adriana. "I said I'm semi-retired, but life seems to have a way of finding me things to do."

Adriana gave a quiet snort and focused on her food.

A big plate mounded high with rice and mutton followed the *mezze*, delicious and fragrant, reminding John of the biriyanis he had eaten in India. They ate while the conversation flowed easily between John and Gunther, Adriana listening and contributing her point of view now and then. Johanna sat quietly, eating, smiling politely. John felt a little sorry for her, unable to join in the conversation although Gunther translated for her from time to time. The other couple remained silent, the wife occasionally glancing in their direction and smiling, but the husband ignored them and puffed away on the *sheesha*, filling the tent with clouds of sweet-scented smoke.

After the meal, Umar reappeared with a large silver samovar with tiny porcelain cups and a bowl of dates.

Kneeling beside them, he poured small servings of hot black coffee, which they sipped while chewing on the sticky sweet dates.

Adriana snuggled in close to John and laid her head on his shoulder as they gazed out over the campfire into the pitch darkness of the desert.

"This is magical." She kissed him on the cheek. "Thank you."

John smiled and put his coffee cup down on the table.

"I'm happy I got to share it with you, *habibi*."

He glanced over at Gunther and Johanna who were having a quiet conversation, then gave Adriana's leg a squeeze.

"Why don't we head back to our tent and see how much more magical we can make this?"

"Mr. Hayes,"—Adriana pulled away in mock shock—"Are you taking advantage of me?"

27

"*C'est eux.* It's them." Bogdan passed the binoculars to the man lying in the sand next to him, who peered through them, adjusting the focus until he could see clearly.

"*Oui,*" he whispered as he watched John and Adriana stand, say their goodbyes to an elderly couple, then walk out of the tent and along the path toward their tent. The darkness was complete, not a light for miles around except from the desert camp. A blanket of stars covered them from above, and a gentle breeze brought cool air across the dunes.

Taha looked away from the eyepiece of the binoculars and peered at the dark shape of the man beside him.

"*La troisième tente à droite.*"

Bogdan nodded although Taha couldn't see him in the darkness. Neither of the men was French, but after five years in the *Légion Étrangère*, the French Foreign Legion, it had become second nature to converse in the language, their only common tongue—neither Taha able to speak Ukrainian nor Bogdan able to speak Arabic—and Taha with only a rudimentary command of English.

He crawled backward, away from the top of the dune, then rolled over onto his back and stared up at the blanket of stars overhead. He heard Taha slide down beside him.

"Let's hit them at sunrise. The client wants a video, so we will need daylight."

"I don't like it. Why wait? Let's get him now."

Bogdan considered Taha's suggestion, thinking over all the permutations. They had seen action together in Mali and Afghanistan and trusted each other, respected each other's opinions, never making a decision until they were both happy with it. It had been the same during their final posting in Abu Dhabi at the ironically named *Camp de la Paix,* Peace Camp, when Bogdan had suggested branching out on their own. They had seen the money made by private contractors in Afghanistan for the same work they were trained to do but paid much less for. It was Bogdan's idea, Taha initially reluctant, scared to leave the security of a monthly paycheck, money he sent back to his family in Algeria. But after many late-night discussions, he agreed, and within a week of Taha finishing his five-year contract with the *Légion,* they had gone into business, setting up the company called *Frontiere Moyen Oriental* Services, or FOM Services as was written on their business cards. At first, business was good, contracts protecting oil pipelines and providing security for foreign clients visiting their businesses in volatile parts of Africa and the Middle East had paid well. But a couple of mistakes—the death of a client in Sudan, unforeseen sabotage of an oil rig—meant business had slowly dried up, forcing the pair to carry out jobs on the grey side of legal—like the one they were tasked to perform now.

Bogdan reached into his shirt pocket and pulled out a packet of Marlboro Reds, shaking one out and glancing over his shoulder to make sure he was out of the line of sight from the desert camp, flicked open his Zippo, and lit the cigarette. He took a long pull, holding the smoke in his lungs, the nicotine giving him a much-needed boost. They had been on the road since that morning, and he was tired. He exhaled the smoke, then spoke.

"The morning is better. If we take him now, we will have to hold him until daylight before we can make the video. The client's terms were very clear, he wants to see him on video. Otherwise, we don't get the rest of the fee." He took another drag from his cigarette. "If we take him now, it gives the others in the camp a chance to seek help while we're still holding him. It's too risky. It's better we go in, take him, finish the job, and get out of here."

"*Oui,* this is correct," Taha nodded slowly. "But what about the others? Do we kill them too?"

Bogdan thought for a moment.

"*Non.*" He took another drag of the cigarette. "We have to get out of the country and back to Dubai. We can't afford there to be a massive manhunt for the killers of a camp filled with tourists. We take him and make it look like he wandered off into the desert and disappeared, then no-one will come looking for us."

"The woman?"

Bogdan flicked ash from the end of his cigarette.

"We'll take her too. Now let's get some food and sleep. We go in at six-thirty."

28

John opened his eyes with a start to darkness. He tried to raise his hands to rub his eyes, but he couldn't move. He wriggled and shifted in panic, realizing his arms and legs were bound. He strained his senses, trying to make sense of the darkness. He appeared to be sitting in a chair, his arms bound behind him, his legs tied to the chair legs. He struggled and tried to loosen his arms and legs, but they were held fast. He took a deep breath, trying to slow his heartbeat, and his lungs filled with hot stale air filled with familiar scents. He racked his memory for when he had smelled them before but couldn't place them. A bead of sweat ran down his forehead and into his left eye, the eye blinking shut against the sting of the salt.

His heart pounded in his chest as he struggled harder to free himself. Something hard and cold pressed against the back of his head, and he moved his head forward, but the object shifted with him. He heard a laugh, and out of the darkness in front of him, three faces appeared, sneering and taunting. They looked familiar—no, it wasn't possible! His body went cold, and he squirmed from side-to-side, trying to get free. The disembodied faces leered, and from behind him, he heard a voice that sent a shiver down his spine.

"Now, it's your turn, motherfucker."

"No, no," John screamed as he heard the click of a firing pin.

29

"John, John, it's okay, it's okay."

He opened his eyes and looked up at Adriana, leaning over him, her long black hair falling either side of her face.

"It's okay, John."

John exhaled slowly, his heart still pounding away in his chest. Adriana stroked his forehead and ran her fingers through his hair.

"You had a bad dream."

John looked around the tent, familiarizing himself, bringing himself back into the present. The tension left his body, and he relaxed. Reaching up, he brushed her hair away from her face.

"Thank you," he smiled. "Yes, it was just a dream." He pulled her down beside him, and she rested her head on his chest. John kissed the top of her head. "Sorry to wake you."

"What was the dream, John?"

"Oh nothing, it didn't make sense." He thought fast. "Maybe the food didn't agree with me. They say cheese before bedtime gives you nightmares, perhaps dates too."

"You seemed really worried. I can still feel your heart beating really fast."

"Don't worry." John stroked her hair. "Get some sleep."

He lay, staring at the roof of the tent, unable to sleep. He hadn't had his nightmares for a long time, thought he had got over them, but he recognized the faces in the dream— three young men from Bangalore, men whose life he had taken in revenge for killing his wife. Why was he seeing them again? It must have been the email from Detective Inspector Rajiv Sampath stirring up long-buried memories from his sub-conscious. He hoped that's all it was. Rajiv had mentioned Surya Patil was in Dubai. It was a strange coincidence he was there at the same time as John and had asked for his file. Why had he done that? John frowned in the darkness. Maybe it was nothing. He sighed. Anyway, he and Adriana had moved on to Oman. There was no way Surya Patil could know where he was now.

30

John lay awake, waiting for the alarm. His heartbeat was finally back to normal, but his t-shirt and boxer shorts were soaked with sweat. Sighing, he looked over at the dark shape of Adriana sleeping beside him, her breathing deep and regular. John rolled over and sat up. He wouldn't be able to sleep again. He reached for the phone on the bedside table, just as the alarm buzzed. Adriana groaned a protest behind him as John killed the alarm and checked the time on the phone—four-thirty a.m. He rubbed his face, then turned and looked back at Adriana.

"*Habibi*," he whispered. "It's time to get up. We have to be ready by five."

Adriana groaned again and pulled the cover over her head.

"Baby." John shook her arm.

"You go," her muffled voice came from under the covers. "I want to sleep."

John scratched his head. He too needed to sleep, his night being less than restful, but he had promised Mansur they would meet him and didn't want to let him down. Plus, he was keen to experience the early morning out in the dunes. He pulled the covers back, exposing Adriana's head and leaned over to kiss her on the cheek.

"Sleep, *habibi*," he whispered, then stood up.

Creeping to the bathroom, he pulled the door closed before turning on the battery-powered lamp. He turned on the tap, allowing a slow trickle of water to flow, then splashed it on his face, waking him up and wiping the sleep from his eyes, before taming his hair with more water. Squeezing paste onto his toothbrush, he brushed his teeth, studying the tired face looking back at him from the mirror. The lamp accentuated the shadows, and the circles around his eyes looked darker than normal, adding years to his life. Spitting the paste into the basin, he rinsed out his mouth. He could always come back for a nap after breakfast.

Keeping the bathroom door slightly open, allowing a thin sliver of light from the bathroom to fall into the sleeping area, he dressed in the clothes he had laid out the night before. Pulling on a light jacket, he picked up his boots with one hand and leaned back into the bathroom and flicked off the light. He let himself out of the tent, pulling the flap closed behind him, crouching down to lace up his boots. The air was crisp and quiet, a complete contrast to the oppressive heat of the day. John tipped his head back and gazed up at the display above him. It was still dark, but high above, the heavens beamed down their blessings in a billion twinkling lights. A satellite streaked across the black expanse and in the distance just above the horizon, a star shone brighter than all the others, the planet Venus heralding the arrival of dawn.

John zipped his jacket and followed the path toward the parked vehicles near the reception building. Noticing a movement in the darkness, he recognized the shape of a man beside three much larger indistinguishable shapes. They shifted and moved as he approached, and it was only when he got closer, he realized what they were.

"Good morning, Mansur. *As salaam aleikum.*"

"*Wa aleikum salaam,* John" Mansur reached out and shook John's hand. "Did you sleep well?"

"Yes, thank you," John lied as he gazed at the three camels standing behind Mansur. "I thought we were taking the Land Cruiser?"

Mansur chuckled. "I thought it would be more fun the traditional way." He looked over John's shoulder. "And Madam?"

"She won't be joining us. She's exhausted." John gestured toward his Land Cruiser. "We've been driving a lot."

"Oh, that's a pity," Mansur shrugged. "But..." His teeth flashed in the darkness. "We can move faster now. I was going to walk."

John raised an eyebrow. "There are three camels?"

"You will see John, you will see. Come."

Mansur tugged on the rope of the leading camel. It groaned in protest, and he muttered a command in Arabic, at the same time swinging the knotted rope end at the camel's knees. Slowly, reluctantly, it dropped to its front knees, then lowered its haunches to the ground.

"Come, John. This one I call Aladdin," he chuckled. "He is yours."

John walked over and with Mansur's help, clambered onto the saddle, then Mansur passed over the rope.

"Hold on to the front of the saddle and lean forward," he instructed and with another command, followed by a clicking sound with his tongue instructed Aladdin to stand up. With a lurch, the camel stood first with the front legs, then the back, John hanging on as the ship of the desert clambered to its feet and stood. Turning its head to look back at John, it let out what sounded like an angry belch.

"Just ignore him, John. Aladdin doesn't like to wake up early. He's a little grumpy, but he is strong and reliable."

John grinned, excited at his first time on a camel, watching as Mansur clicked his tongue at the other camel. It stepped forward and after a simple muttered command from Mansur, lowered itself to the ground. Mansur—with much more agility than John had shown—seated himself with ease, and the camel climbed to its feet.

"What is your camel called?" John asked.

Mansur laughed. "This is Angelina."

"Angelina?"

"Yes, after Angelina Jolie because she is so beautiful, no?"

"I'm not sure Angelina would appreciate having a camel named after her," John laughed. John saw Mansur's shoulders shrug in the dim light.

"Why not? It is an honor."

John grinned. He wished Adriana was with him. He must remember to tell her about Angelina later.

Mansur nudged the camel forward and led John away from the parked cars and into the desert, the third camel following quietly behind.

31

Bogdan stirred, pulled his arm out of the sleeping bag, and peered at the luminous dial on his watch—his internal alarm clock never let him down. Unzipping the sleeping bag, he sat up and glanced over at the form lying on the foam mat beside him.

"Taha," he murmured. "It's time."

Taha sat bolt upright, still in the sleeping bag and looked around. Years of sleeping rough in the deserts of the Middle East and Africa had inured them to discomfort, and they were both instantly alert

"You pack up the camp, I'll prepare coffee and food. It will be a long day."

"*Oui.*"

The two men switched on head torches and busied themselves with a routine they had performed hundreds of times in the service of the *Légion*. The only difference now, it was in the service of their bank balance.

Bogdan set up the camp stove and brewed strong coffee while Taha rolled up the bedrolls and squared them away in the SUV.

Once the coffee was ready, they sat cross-legged on the sand, facing each other, sipping the hot, heavily sweetened liquid as they stripped and cleaned their weapons on a sheet laid out between them.

Both men were carrying the PAMAS G1, the French made version of the Beretta 92 semi-automatic. It wasn't the best weapon, as the slide had a reputation for breaking after continuous use, but it was one they were familiar with. Standard issue in the *Légion* and easily obtainable, these weapons had disappeared out the back door while they were serving, never to be found again by the garrison quartermaster. Chambered for 9mm and fitted with fifteen-round, sand-resistant magazines, they held more than enough ammunition for the task they had in mind.

32

The two men rode for about an hour, Mansur leading them down a well-traveled vehicle track before heading into the dunes. The stars above faded as the sky lightened in the pre-dawn, the dark shape of the dunes transforming into beautifully sculpted waves of sand. The air was still cool, and apart from the creak of the saddle leather and the occasional grumble from Aladdin, there was silence all around. As John rocked back-and-forth in the see-saw motion of the camel's gait, he couldn't help but feel awe at the beauty that surrounded him. He could understand why explorers of old were drawn back to the desert—the vast open spaces and the all-encompassing silence of it all. It was stunning, and his chest swelled with emotion. He regretted not forcing Adriana to wake up and share the experience with him.

"Have you always lived here?" he asked, glancing over at Mansur.

"For most of my life, yes." Mansur looked back and smiled, shifting his position, so he was sitting sideways. "My family has lived here for as long as anyone can remember. But times are changing," he shrugged. "The young people prefer to move to the cities. It's not an easy life here."

"Did you ever feel like moving?"

"I did. I went to university in Muscat. The government helps us a lot, wanting to educate us, but..." He trailed off and gazed around at the desert. "I couldn't live in the city." He waved his arm at the dunes. "I missed this. In the city, everyone is in a hurry, everyone is angry. There is so much noise, there is no beauty." Looking back at John, he continued, "Here is where I'm happy." Pulling a face, he shrugged, "But my daughters? I don't know what they will do."

He turned back and faced the front, and they rode on in silence for a while before Mansur called out, *"Yalla,* we're almost there. Just in time." He clicked his tongue, said something in Arabic, urging Angelina into a trot.

Aladdin groaned and trotted after them, John hanging on for dear life. Mansur led them up the side of a large dune, then as they crested it, he slowed, and John's mouth dropped open.

All around them, in every direction, was a rippling golden sea. On the far horizon, the first rays of the sun were just making their appearance, turning the sky orange and red, the waves of the dunes changing color in unison.

Mansur pulled his camel to a stop, and it lowered itself to the ground. Climbing off, he walked over to John, instructing Aladdin to do the same. Aladdin grumbled but did so, and John climbed off and twisted and stretched away the discomfort, the inside of his legs and his hips sore, unused to the motion of the camel. Mansur walked to the third camel and once it was sitting on the sand, unloaded it. Now in the light, John could see it was laden with supplies. He watched as Mansur spread a beautiful rug on the sand.

"Can I help?" asked John.

"No, please make yourself comfortable, enjoy the sunrise."

John sat down on the rug and removed his phone from his pocket, clicking a couple of pictures of the view to share with Adriana later.

Mansur set a large bag, woven from goat's wool, down on the rug, knelt beside it, and started unpacking. He removed a flask, a silver plate, and a Tupperware box, laying them on the rug.

"Not everything is traditional," he said, winking at John. "We have to move with the times."

He took out two packages wrapped in newspaper and unwrapped them, removing two small porcelain cups. Opening the flask, he poured steaming black coffee into both before handing one to John, then opened the plastic box and took out a big lump of sticky sweet dates and placed them on the silver tray. "Desert breakfast," he grinned.

"Fantastic, thank you."

Sitting beside John, he raised his cup, nodded at John, and took a sip.

"Just in time. Look."

John followed Mansur's gaze and watched as a thin golden line appeared on the horizon, then slowly but steadily, the line transformed into a semi-circle of fire, spreading orange, pink, and red rays of light across the sand. John placed his cup down and picked up his phone, clicking photos to share later, but sadly, none of them did justice to the awesome sight before them. He put the phone away, preferring to imprint the sight in his memory. The two men sat in complete silence, enjoying the beautiful beginning of the day, not a care in the world, not a thought of the past or the future. For the first time, for as long as John could remember, he felt content, the memory of his nightmare forgotten.

33

Bogdan glanced once more around the camp, checking everything was packed away, then checked his watch. It was time.

Looking toward the top of the dune where Taha was lying, staring through the binoculars at the desert camp, he gave a low whistle. Taha turned, looked back, then slid back down the face of the dune toward Bogdan.

"All good. The camp is quiet. All the guests are still sleeping. The only movement is in the kitchen."

"*Bon.* Let's go." Bogdan removed the PAMAS G1 from his waistband, checked it quickly, then slid it back. It didn't need checking, he had cleaned and oiled it thoroughly that morning, but it was a habit of his whenever he went into action, and it comforted him.

They climbed into the cab of the SUV, and Bogdan started the engine. Glancing over at Taha, he nodded, then slowly pulled out of their camp.

John and Adriana's tent was the furthest tent from the reception and kitchen buildings. It took about thirty minutes before they could approach the camp from that direction. They wanted to avoid detection by the staff, just slip in and out quietly, but they also needed to get the vehicle as close as possible. The client wanted a video of the execution, so they couldn't do it in the camp.

Bogdan kept the revs low, conscious the sound of an engine would carry far in the desert. Once in sight of the camp, Bogdan reduced the speed even more, crawling toward John and Adriana's tent. He turned the Land Cruiser in a wide circle, then backed it toward the tent, ready for a quick getaway. With a quick glance at Taha, he climbed out and eased the door closed.

Both men pulled *shemaghs* up around their faces and removed their weapons from their waistbands before proceeding cautiously to the tent. Standing either side of the tent door, Bogdan once again looked at Taha and nodded. Taha quietly opened the tent door and slipped inside, Bogdan close on his heels, Taha moving to the left, Bogdan to the right. Bogdan approached the bed and frowned—there was only one body in the bed. He glanced across at Taha and flicked his head toward the bathroom door. Taha understood and stepped quietly to the bathroom, paused, then with his weapon at the ready, pushed open the door with his left hand. He waited for any response from inside, then stepped in and looked around.

Bogdan waited, his pistol still trained on the shape in the bed until Taha stepped out and shook his head.

Bogdan clenched his jaw, stepped over to the bed, and in one movement, pulled the cover off the sleeping form. He stepped back, both men pointing their weapons at the bed.

Adriana stirred and rolled over.

"John?" She blinked her eyes open, gasped at the sight of the two men, and scrambled toward the back of the bed.

Bogdan held his finger to his lips, warning her to be quiet as she sat upright and pulled the sheet over her.

She struggled for words, her mouth moving open and closed, no sound coming out until finally, she could put words together.

"Wh-wh-what do you want??"

34

The sun was now above the horizon, the dunes losing their multicolored hues but still beautiful in the long shadows of the dawn. John heard a chirp and watched as a tiny black and white bird flew back-and-forth around them, hovering in front as if looking at them before darting off to one side, only to return a moment later.

"A Hume's Wheatear," said Mansur. "It's very common here."

"How does it survive out here?"

"The desert is full of life, John, you just need to know where to look." He stood up. "*Yalla*, come. I'll show you."

Mansur led John across the sand, his eyes scanning the surface of the dunes until he stopped and crouched down. John squatted beside him and looked at a trail of tiny footprints leading across the face of the dune.

"See this? Cheesman's Gerbil. It spends the days underground and comes out at night." He stood and walked on. After a moment, he stopped and beckoned John enthusiastically.

"John, look at this." He pointed down at a set of paw prints. "This is a sand fox. It's small, about this big." He held his hands apart to show the size.

"Like a small dog?"

"Yes," Mansur nodded. "But it has big ears to keep it cool."

"Wow, I always thought the desert was lifeless."

"No, John. It's tough, but these creatures have adapted to survive here. Just like my own people have done for hundreds of years."

"It's an incredible place, Mansur. You're fortunate to have experienced this. For most people, life is lived in a concrete jungle, devoid of life with no connection to nature. Most people will never see anything like this."

"Yes, John, you're right." Mansur gazed across the desert landscape, a wistful look in his eyes. "I don't think my daughters' children will ever have the experiences I've had." He turned back and looked John in the eye. "My people are losing their connection with their home. All they want now is a new car and a TV. Our ways are being lost."

"I fear it's happening worldwide, Mansur."

"Yes," Mansur shrugged. "Perhaps you are right."

He looked up at the sun. "Come, we should head back. It won't be long before the heat becomes uncomfortable for you."

The two men walked back to the resting camels and packed up the picnic, Mansur showing John how to stow the items and make the camel bag secure on the pack camel. He took one last look around the sand, making sure nothing was left behind, then turned to John.

"Ready?"

"Yes,"

"Come."

He helped John mount up, then with a command, instructed the grumbling Aladdin to get to his feet. Mansur climbed onboard his camel and once on her feet, guided her back toward the camp, John and the pack camel falling in behind.

"Thank you, Mansur," John called out. "This was a wonderful experience. How do you say it? *Shukraan jazilan?*"

Mansur looked back and laughed.

"Yes, John, correct. *Shukraan jazilan.* Thank you very much. I will make a Bedouin of you yet."

They rode in silence, enjoying the surroundings. John got used to the camel's rocking motion and found it soothing, the rhythmical back-and-forth motion and the silence making him drowsy after his early start and poor night's sleep. He could feel his eyes drooping shut when a question from Mansur caught his attention.

"Can you hear that?"

John strained his ears, hearing nothing until...

"Yes, I hear it. An engine?"

"Yes, a vehicle is coming."

They rode on, listening as the vehicle noise grew louder, the revs rising and falling as the vehicle struggled for traction.

A white SUV appeared over the crest of a far dune, and Mansur shaded his eyes with his hand, looking into the distance.

"A tourist vehicle. "

"How can you tell?"

"See the red number plates?"

John stared, but the vehicle was too far for him to see the plates, let alone anything red. Mansur had far superior eyesight.

"It's unusual for one to be this far out."

Both men watched as the vehicle neared, then pulled to a stop in front of them. Mansur reined his camel to a halt, Aladdin and the pack camel stopping behind him. The angle of the sun on the windscreen prevented him from seeing inside, and they watched as the door opened and a man stepped out. John narrowed his eyes—he looked familiar.

"As salaam aleikum. Are you lost?" Mansur asked.

The man ignored him, looking straight at John.

"John Hayes? I suggest you don't go back to the camp."

35

"*Merde,*" Bogdan cursed. "Where is he?"

Adriana shook her head, looking back-and-forth between the two men, her eyes wide in panic.

He stepped closer, raising the gun until it pointed between her eyes.

"I said, where is he?"

Adriana flinched and turned her head away.

"I-I-I don't know."

"Don't lie. He is your boyfriend, where is he?" Bogdan growled.

"He... he...." despite her panic, Adriana thought fast. Who were these guys? She couldn't tell them where John had gone. "He's gone into Bidiyah. To get medicine. I have an upset stomach."

Bogdan stepped closer and ground the barrel into Adriana's temple. She cried out, a mixture of fear and pain.

"If you are lying..." He left the threat open and looked over at Taha. "Secure her."

Taha lowered his weapon, tucked it into his waistband,

then from the pocket of his cargo pants, removed a handful of cable ties. Bogdan stepped back, giving Taha room to work, but kept his weapon trained on the woman.

Taha grabbed Adriana by the arm and pulled her to him, forcing her onto her stomach. Grabbing both arms, he secured her wrists behind her back. With another pair of cable ties, he fastened her ankles together. Then he rolled her over and from his other pocket, removed a roll of duct tape, tearing off a strip. Adriana's eyes widened in fear.

"No, no, I'll be quiet."

Taha ignored her and stuck the strip across her mouth. When he finished, both men stepped away and moved toward the door.

"What do we do?" Taha asked in a low voice

Bogdan looked down at Adriana, lying on the bed, shaking his head.

"We wait. He'll come back." He looked up at Taha. "Move the vehicle. He mustn't see it when he comes back."

"D'accord," Taha nodded. He moved to open the tent flap and stopped as Bogdan placed a hand on his arm.

"Go check if their vehicle is still parked by the reception. Be careful, no-one can know we are here."

Taha nodded and walked out.

Bogdan turned back to look at the bed and frowned. Shit. Years of experience had taught him things rarely went as planned, but he still hated it. He did a mental calculation. If he allowed a one-and-a-half-hour journey each way to Bidiyah, plus another half hour for John Hayes to buy the medicine, that meant three-and-a-half-hours. He looked at his watch—he must have left at least half an hour earlier, perhaps an hour at the most. That meant they would have to wait two-and-a-half to three hours before he returned. Risky. The chances of them being found were higher the longer they stayed in the camp. He shook his head, his fingers tightening around the grip of the weapon. Damn it. He willed himself to relax.

He'd already outlaid a lot of money on this mission, and the client wouldn't pay the rest until they did the job. There was nothing they could do but wait. Walking over to the camp chair, he moved it to the corner, away from the entrance, positioning it so he had a clear line of sight but wouldn't be visible to whoever came in. Sitting down, he laid the handgun on his lap and crossed his legs at the ankles. He had spent most of his career in the *Légion* waiting for action—this was nothing new.

36

John narrowed his eyes. "You were at the Turtle Sanctuary."

The man nodded, put his hands on his hips, and sighed. "It's a long story."

Mansur looked back-and-forth between the two men, puzzled. "Is everything okay, John?"

John didn't take his eyes off the man standing in front of them. He was in early middle-age but looked older, his neck and face deeply lined, especially around the eyes, as if he'd spent years squinting against the sun. Sunspots covered his arms, and he pronounced his 'i's as 'e's, suggesting he was Australian. That would explain the sun damage to his skin. His clothes were rumpled, his face unshaven, his hair a tangled mess.

"I don't know, Mansur." Addressing the man, he asked, "Who are you?"

"My name is Steve Jones. Mr. Surya Patil hired me to follow you."

John's heart sank.

"Fuck." He cursed quietly.

Mansur looked on with concern but said nothing.

"And why shouldn't I go back to the camp?"

"Look, mate,"—Steve spread his hands wide—"I don't know what's going on between you, but this Patil guy has sent two men to the camp. They looked dodgy, and I got a bad feeling about it, so I followed them."

John's stomach churned.

"Where are they now?"

"I saw them drive into the camp this morning. They camped in the desert overnight. I've been watching them."

"Adriana! Mansur, we have to go now!"

John swung the end of his guide rope and whacked Aladdin on the rump. The camel groaned loudly and looked back in protest. John swung the rope again and kicked the sides of his camel, urging it forward. It took a step forward.

"Wait," Steve cried out, raising his hands. "They're armed."

John stopped urging the camel on, and Aladdin stopped walking.

"I saw them cleaning their weapons this morning," Steve continued. "They both have semi-automatic pistols."

"Arrrrrgh," John roared. Leaping from the camel, he landed in the sand, took a step forward, stumbled in the deep sand, falling to his knees. He jumped up and ran toward the Pajero.

"Give me your keys," he demanded.

Steve held his hands up and gripped John by the shoulders.

"Wait, wait. You can't go charging in like that. I told you, they're armed. I've seen them. They look professional."

John struggled to get free, frustrated, but he knew Steve was right. Steve relaxed his grip, and John pulled himself free, turned, and kicked the front tire of the Pajero, his eyes hot with tears, his face flushed with anger.

"Fuck, fuck, fuck, fucking motherfuckers!" he screamed. Again and again, he kicked the tire until finally, his energy spent, he leaned with both hands on the front wing of the Pajero, his head hanging, his chest and shoulders heaving up and down with the exertion. Getting a grip on himself, he turned and glared at Steve.

"You brought them here. You told them where I am."

Steve didn't back down and glowered back at him.

"Yes, I did. I was paid to do a job." He raised his hands to the side. "But I didn't know these guys were coming. I'm helping you now, aren't I?"

"Why?"

Steve exhaled. "Mate..."

"I'm not your mate."

"Yeah... look I'm an ex-cop, fifteen years on the Australian Police Force. Now, I'm a private investigator. I get paid to follow people, find out what they are up to, who they're shagging. I thought that's what you were doing, shagging Patil's woman, but..." he shrugged. "I can see you're a nice guy. That you love each other. I can't imagine her with Patil." He glanced at Mansur, then back again. "Then I thought you'd taken money from him, but when I met those guys, I knew something was off. I don't know what you've done, mate, but I'm not gonna be a part of someone getting hurt."

John nodded. The guy seemed genuine. Could he trust him?

"You said they were already at the camp?"

"Yeah. I watched them drive down and enter the camp from the back. They're in your tent, mate."

"Fuck!" John clenched his fist and turning, slammed it down on the wing of the SUV. "Bastards!"

He felt a hand on his arm and turned to look into Mansur's concerned face.

"John, I'll help you. We'll save her."

John nodded, gritted his teeth, and turned to face Steve.

"Well, Mr. P.I., you brought them here. Any ideas?"

37

Bogdan stiffened as he heard footsteps. Picking up his weapon, he aimed at the entrance as the door opened. Taha poked his head inside, unable to see Bogdan, his eyes still adjusting after the bright light outside. Bogdan relaxed.

"Over here," he whispered.

Taha looked in his direction, then slipped inside and walked over, glancing at Adriana on the bed as he did so.

"She's lying. All the cars are still there."

"*Salope!* Bitch." He stood and strode to the bed, ripping the duct tape off Adriana's face. She gasped, her eyes watering, and struggled to move away. Bogdan cocked his weapon, grabbed her by the hair, and stuffed the barrel into her mouth. Tears streamed down cheeks, her chin trembling as she struggled for breath.

Bogdan leaned down, his face inches from her and growled, "Where is he?"

Adriana's eyes opened wider, her eyes darting from Bogdan to Taha and back, but with the barrel in her mouth, all she could manage was a groan.

He pulled the barrel out and tugged harder on her hair, pulling her head up off the bed.

"Where is he?"

Adriana swallowed, her breath coming in fits and starts.

"I don't know, I don't know."

"Bullshit! If you lie to me once more, I will let my friend here,"—he looked over his shoulder at Taha standing behind him—"have some fun with you."

Adriana shook her head, "No, no."

"It's up to you. Now tell me, where is he?"

"I told you, I don't know."

Bogdan screwed up his face and tightened his grip on her hair, pulling her head back until the veins stood out on her neck.

"H-h-he... w-w-went this morning to look at the sunrise, but I don't know where. I'm telling the truth."

Bogdan dropped her head on the bed and stood back, his pistol hanging by his side. Adriana lay there, her head turned away from him, her chest rising and falling as she sobbed.

Bogdan picked up the duct tape strip, pulled her face toward him, and stuck it back over her mouth before turning to Taha. Taha looked at him questioningly as Bogdan stared back, his mind whirring away, calculating the odds, running over the different scenarios.

He signaled toward the door, and stepping over, they lowered their voices, switching back to French so Adriana couldn't understand.

"We have to wait for him. We don't get paid for the woman. Only the man."

"It's risky, though. The longer we stay here, the more chance we'll get caught."

Bogdan puffed out his cheeks. "But what can the people

do here? You've seen them. They are civilians. No match for us."

"Hmm," Taha paused while he thought. "I agree. We need the money."

"*Oui*. I say we wait here out of sight, just like we were going to. Actually, it's better. We don't have to wait three hours for him to come back from Bidiyah. He could be back anytime now."

"*Oui.*"

Bogdan clasped Taha's arm.

"I want you to watch the tent from the outside. Find somewhere to lie, up, out of sight. I'll wait in here. When you see him come in, you follow immediately after him. We'll secure him, then take him out to the desert and make the video." He squeezed Taha's arm. "*D'accord?*"

"*D'accord.*"

"*Allez.*"

Bogdan turned and looked back at Adriana on the bed as Taha left the tent. Hopefully, this would all be over with soon.

Walking over, he looked down at her. She was a beauty this one. He placed the end of the barrel on her knee and smiled when she flinched away. He slid the barrel up her leg, pushing the hem of her negligee higher, exposing the smooth olive skin of her inner thigh. He licked his lips, one side of his mouth curling upward in a lecherous sneer. Maybe the job would have some extra perks.

38

The three men lay prone on top of the dune, staring down at the camp about one kilometer away. It was as close as they could approach without risk of being seen. Smoke rose from the kitchen building, and they could see the figures of Fouad and Umar moving back-and-forth between the building and the large tent that served as the dining area, making preparations for breakfast. Everything looked normal. Movement outside one of the tents caught their eye, and they watched as Gunther stepped outside, his tall thin figure wrapped in a dressing gown. He looked around, stretched, then walked back inside the tent.

"Where are the bastards?" John growled.

Neither of the other men said anything, unable to see any sign of the men. He heard Mansur curse in Arabic and stiffen as a tiny figure ran out of the staff quarters, followed a short while later by another, the faint sound of laughter carrying to them on the breeze. They chased each other before disappearing behind a tent.

"My daughters."

"Are you sure they're in the camp?" John looked over at Steve.

"Yeah." Steve rolled onto his back and pinched the bridge of his nose. "I saw them drive in, mate."

"Then where is their vehicle?" John asked. "Look at the carpark. There are only three cars. One of them is mine."

"I don't know, mate. All I can tell you is what I saw. I don't know where they are now."

"How do I know you aren't making all this up?"

"Come on, man," Steve sighed. "I just spent the night sleeping in my car in the fucking desert. What's in it for me to make this up?"

John felt a hand on his arm then heard Mansur's low voice.

"John. Which tent is yours?"

"The one closest to us."

Mansur shaded his eyes and studied the sand around the tent.

"See there." He pointed. "Vehicle tracks are there."

John looked but couldn't see anything.

"Bloody hell, mate, you've got the eyes of an eagle," replied Steve who was lying on his front again, looking toward the camp. "All I can see is sand."

Mansur continued staring, his eyes running back-and-forth across the sand.

"There," he pointed. "The tracks lead that way."

He turned to make sure John could see where he was pointing, but he wasn't there. Puzzled, he looked over his shoulder to see John running down the face of the dune behind him.

He sprang to his feet, hitched the hem of his *dishdasha*

high above his knees, and sprinted down the dune after him, leaving Steve alone at the top of the dune, wondering where everyone had gone.

39

John couldn't think straight, filled with rage. Someone had tracked him into the desert and taken Adriana from him. He spread his arms wide for balance as he struggled to keep his footing, his legs sinking up to the knees as he descended the soft sand face of the dune, sand cascading past him in a golden avalanche. He would find the bastards and make them suffer. John stumbled and fell, throwing his arms out in front to break his fall. He landed face first in the sand, then tumbled head over heels until the sand leveled out. He lay there, catching his breath, spitting sand from his mouth. A puff of foul-smelling air crossed his face, and he blinked his eyes open to see Aladdin peering down at him. The sand beside him shifted, and Mansur appeared, gasping for breath. With a wave of his hand, he shooed the camel away, then bent over and rested his hands on his knees, catching his breath.

"John, wait," he blurted between breaths.

John sat up, and Mansur reached out a hand. He allowed himself to be pulled to his feet, and Mansur clasped him by both shoulders.

"John, you have to calm down."

"No." John shook his hands off his shoulders. "I have to stop them. They have Adriana."

"I know, John." Mansur held up both hands in a placatory gesture. "But we'll do this together." He waved his arms, showing the sandy expanse around them, "Look around you, John. It's not the beach. It's the desert. You will die here."

John said nothing, gritting his teeth, and looked down at his feet.

"You don't have water, you don't have shade. It's only eight o'clock now, but you can already feel the heat." He reached out and touched John's arm. "Trust me, John. I will help you, but we stick together."

John looked up at Mansur, the young Bedouin's forehead creased, his eyes steady and focused on John.

"Okay."

"Good."

They both turned to watch Steve make his way down the dunes.

"You two lovers made up then?"

40

John watched as Mansur raised his finger to his lips, quieting them both. They listened for a while, but the only sound was the breathing from the camels.

"I can't hear any vehicle," Mansur spoke after a while. "Sound carries across the desert, and if a vehicle was moving, we would hear something."

"I can't hear a thing, mate," agreed Steve.

"Do you think they've just hidden it behind the dunes?" asked John, ignoring him.

Mansur scrunched his face up as he thought.

"Yes. There is nothing in that direction. If they've taken your wife, it wouldn't make sense to go that way."

John ignored the wife reference and nodded.

"That means they're waiting for me." John exhaled loudly and put his hands on his hips, chewing his lip as he thought. Looking up, he continued. "I don't know what to do. I can't leave Adriana."

"Mate, there are two of them. There's three of us," said Steve. "We can beat them."

"But how? You said they're armed. Do you have a weapon in your Pajero?"

"No, mate," Steve shrugged.

"Yeah, I thought so. We're fucked." John looked at Mansur, who was standing beside his camel, stroking its neck. "We can't stay out here, you said so yourself. We'll die. And if I don't go back, they'll hurt Adriana."

Mansur listened calmly, then gave a half smile.

"We won't die yet, John. We have water and dates." He turned to Steve, "Mr...?"

"Steve."

"Mr. Steve, do you have water and food in your car?"

"Just Steve. I've got half a liter of water left and some biscuits. Sorry, I ate the rest last night."

"It's okay."

"So, we have enough for a day, maybe two?" asked John.

"Yes."

"Hmm, okay," John replied, not convinced they would be okay. "But it doesn't solve the main problem."

"No, but we have some, how do you say in English? Breathing room?" Mansur's face lit up in a grin. "I know. Let's find their vehicle. They'll have supplies too."

"Yes. Okay." John clutched at the faint ray of hope.

Mansur turned to Steve. "We go on foot. Your car will make too much noise." He crossed to his camel and reached into a bag fastened to her saddle and pulled out a red and white *shemagh*, tossing it to Steve. "Cover your head and face. It will get hot." He nodded to John. "You do the same."

John unwrapped his *shemagh* from his neck and attempted to tie it around his head in the same fashion as Mansur.

"Let me." Mansur took it from John, folded it into a large triangle, then reached up and expertly tied it around John's head, covering his hair and the back of his neck. The effect was instant, the green and black checked cloth cutting out the heat and providing much-needed protection. Mansur did the same for Steve.

"Bring your water and any food." He instructed each of the camels to stand up, passing Aladdin's lead rope to John, then took the water and biscuits from Steve, stowing them in the bag on the pack camel. Looking at Steve, he said. "We leave the Pajero here. Don't worry," he continued, noticing Steve's look of concern, "I'll bring you back later."

Taking Angelina's rope in his hand, he looked at both men again and satisfied, said,

"*Yalla*, let's go."

41

The men and three camels walked away from the parked Pajero, Mansur leading the way, John following, Steve taking up the rear. The sun was climbing fast now, the heat rapidly increasing. John removed his light jacket, rolled up the sleeves on his shirt and undid another button, grateful he had worn linen, and even more grateful for the *shemagh* he had bought in a souvenir shop. He glanced back at Steve, who was trudging along behind him. He seemed like a decent guy—he had, after all, come back to warn him when he could be safe in a bar in Dubai sipping on a cold beer—but John still wasn't sure. The residual anger that Steve had been following him still hadn't worn off. John reached up and gave Aladdin a pat on the neck and was rewarded with a grumble, followed by another foul belch.

Mansur led them around the dunes, keeping low, not climbing them, to avoid being spotted. The route zigzagged back-and-forth, and John soon lost complete track of the direction they were traveling. Once again, he looked over his shoulder, reassuring himself if they got lost, he could follow the trail of footprints back to the Pajero. After thirty minutes, Mansur signaled to stop and waited for them to catch up. John's legs were trembling with the exertion of walking through the deep sand. He liked to think he was fit, his legs strong from daily runs, but he had struggled to keep pace with Mansur, whose calves were like steel after a lifetime in the desert. Steve had fallen even further back, and it gave John time to catch his breath and shake the lactic acid out of his legs. Steve arrived, his face red, his breath labored, and Mansur gave him a moment before asking, "Okay?"

Steve nodded and grinned but said nothing.

Mansur glanced up at the sun again, then gestured toward a large dune towering above them.

"I'm going up to take a look. You two wait here." Reaching into the saddlebag, he pulled out Steve's bottle of water. "Take a sip. Not too much." He passed it over, then handing the camel's lead rope to John, hitched up his *dishdasha* and started climbing.

John lowered himself into the shade made by the camels and sat in the sand. Steve walked over and joined him, wiping the sweat from his face with the end of his *shemagh*.

"It won't be much fun later if it's this hot now."

John said nothing, instead watching Mansur climb.

"Tell me, John, why is Surya Patil after you? Did you shag his wife? His daughter?"

John ignored him and watched Mansur, high in the sand above, reach the top and lie prone in the sand.

"He's bloody angry with you, mate," Steve persisted. "He paid me a lot of money to follow you around." He nodded in the general direction of the camp. "And these two thugs won't be cheap. Did you steal from him?"

John narrowed his eyes and slowly turned to look at Steve.

"It's none of your business."

"No skin off my nose mate," Steve shrugged. "But you don't strike me as a criminal."

John turned back to watch Mansur.

"Suit yourself."

"Why are you helping me, Steve? What's the real reason?" John asked, his eyes still on Mansur.

Steve scooped a handful of sand and watched it run through his fingers.

"I told you before. Something about this seems off. I'm an ex-cop." He looked over at John. "It's in my blood. I'm not a bad guy, John, and I don't think you are either."

"I've done some bad things," John spoke so quietly, Steve struggled to hear him.

"That surprises me."

John glanced over at Steve, then looked away again as Mansur headed back down the dune. John got to his feet and dusted the sand off his butt as Mansur reached them.

"Well?"

Mansur grinned. "I've found their vehicle, a Land Cruiser. It's parked at the bottom of the dune. We can get to it but..."

"But what?"

"One of the men is at the top of the dune, watching the camp."

42

"So, how do we do this?" John wiped sweat from his nose, blew out a puff of air through pursed lips, and turned to Steve, "You're sure there are only two of them?"

"Yeah, mate. Just the two of them."

"So, we can assume one is in the camp, waiting for me." John paced back-and-forth as Steve and Mansur looked on.

"We could take out this guy and increase our odds."

Mansur made a face. "That won't be easy, John. He's at the top of the dune. Even approaching him from the rear, there's a big chance he'll notice us coming, then we have nowhere to hide. If he has a gun, then..." He left the sentence open, no need to be specific about the likely consequences.

"We can't approach the camp either without being spotted by the guy on the dune, and the guy in the camp will see anyone approaching." John's shoulders slumped in defeat. "We're screwed either way." He kicked at the sand. "Fuck!" Turning back to the two men, he said, "I can't leave her there, guys. I have to save her."

Mansur looked up at the sun then back at John.

"There might be a way."

"How?"

"We wait."

"For what?"

"For night. When no-one can see us."

John looked at Steve in exasperation, then turned back to Mansur. "Wait out here. It's already baking hot, what will it be like in the middle of the day? You already said we could die out here."

"John, you have to trust me," Mansur smiled reassuringly. "This is my land, I know what to do."

"Okay," John shrugged. "But what about Adriana? We can't leave her there with the other man."

"And we don't have enough water," Steve spoke up.

"We have enough for Bedouin, but you will struggle," Mansur grinned. "But there will be water in their Land Cruiser."

John nodded slowly. "Can we get to it without the lookout on the dune noticing?"

"I think so."

"What if it's locked?" Steve asked.

"I doubt it," Mansur shook his head. "He's parked it out of sight but will need to move fast. Why would he lock it? There's no-one else around."

"It's a chance worth taking," John agreed. "We have no other options at the moment. But it still doesn't solve the problem of leaving Adriana with the other man."

"No, mate," replied Steve, "but Mansur's right. With more water at least we will have some flexibility to work out what to do."

John sighed, thinking for a moment while the other two watched.

"Okay, let's do it." He looked at Steve. "You go to the top of the dune and keep a lookout. If something happens to us..." he shrugged. "Please try to save Adriana."

Steve nodded and patted John on the shoulder.

John gave a half smile.

"Mansur, you and I will go to their vehicle. Let's see what they've got. Hopefully, water and..."—he squinted up at the sun—"some shelter."

"Inshallah," replied Mansur. "God willing."

"Inshallah," Steve repeated, but John said nothing.

John had experienced too much horror and heartbreak to believe in God, and he wasn't about to put his trust in him now. The only one who could save Adriana was John.

43

The two men lay flat on their bellies while behind them the pack camel sat quietly in the sand, its jaw working away on some invisible food. Parked on a flat area about fifty meters away from them was the Land Cruiser. Above them, high on the top of a dune, they could make out the figure of a man lying prone on the sand, keeping watch on the camp through a pair of binoculars.

"I'll go, John." Mansur turned his head to look at John. "If he sees me, he'll just think I'm a thieving Arab. They all think that."

"No, my friend," John shook his head. "I will do it. It's because of me these men have come. You have two daughters. They need you."

Before Mansur could disagree, John pushed himself to his feet and sprinted across the sand, keeping low to remain less visible.

"Al'ama," Mansur cursed and looked up toward the man on the top of the dune, hoping he wouldn't turn around.

John kept low, pumping his arms to help make his way quickly through the soft sand. His feet sank with each step, slowing him down, his thighs burning with the effort. He stumbled and fell but pushed himself to his feet, forcing himself on until finally, he collapsed in the sand beside the Land Cruiser, out of sight of the man on the dune. Sucking in air, he struggled to regain his breath. Looking back at Mansur, he gave him a thumbs up. Mansur raised a hand in reply and continued watching the man on the dune.

John turned and reached up to the door handle. He took a deep breath, hoping the vehicle was unlocked, then pulled on the handle—the door clicked and opened. John let out his breath and got to his knees, opening the door just wide enough for his body to fit and climbed inside, pulling the door closed behind him.

Despite the tinted windows, the interior of the vehicle was hot and stuffy. He reached up and turned off the interior light. It was unlikely someone would see the light through the tint, but John wasn't prepared to take any chances. Looking around, he saw there was nothing on the front seat. He opened the glove compartment, finding paper maps and the service book but nothing of use. A half-full plastic bottle of water rested in the cup holder, and John removed it, unscrewed the cap and took a sip. The water was tepid and tasted of plastic, but John couldn't afford to be fussy. It was already over thirty degrees Celsius outside and climbing. He glanced through the window toward the top of the dune. The man was still lying in place, giving no sign he had seen or heard him. John was grateful for the dark-tinted glass.

John slipped between the front seats to get a closer look at two duffel bags on the back seat. Opening the first one, he found a few items of clothing, a toilet kit, and a pouch at the bottom. John removed and unzipped it, finding a wallet and a passport. John put the pouch back in the bag; he would check them later. Removing the toilet kit, he dropped it on the floor of the car. He looked through the clothing for anything useful, but there was nothing, so he threw them on the floor on top of the toilet kit. Sliding the other bag toward him, he opened it, removed the clothing and toiletries, keeping a wide-brimmed sun hat, which he transferred to the other bag. Another travel pouch was inside, and he put that in the first bag as well. At the bottom of the bag was a box of 9mm rounds which he also transferred. That only confirmed what they already knew; the two men were armed.

Taking another quick look at the top of the dune, he then peered over the back seat into the trunk area. An opened cardboard box, half filled with bottled water caught his eye first. He reached over and transferred the bottles into the kit bag. There were seven bottles, plus the half-full one from the front seat. That should keep them going for a while. There were two foam sleeping rolls which he ignored but took a canvas fly sheet and stuffed that into the second bag. It could be useful for shade.

He glanced up at the dune again and stiffened as he saw the man change position. John held his breath and waited, but the man remained where he was. John breathed out. He had been lucky so far but had to get a move on. He pulled over a second cardboard box and looked inside—a small camp stove with a gas bottle, matches, coffee, a bag of dates, and two boxes of energy bars. These guys didn't seem to eat much. He transferred everything into the second bag and zipped it closed. Swiveling around, he hefted the bag onto the driver's seat, doing the same with the bag full of water bottles. They were heavy. He hoped he could manage both in the run back across the sand. As he climbed through, he caught sight of the car key fob in one of the lower cubby holes on the dashboard. He stifled a chuckle—perfect. Pocketing the key fob, he took another glance toward the top of the dune. Confident the man wasn't looking in his direction, he pushed the passenger door open with his foot and slid out backward until his feet touched the sand. Reaching across the seat, he pulled the first bag toward him, sliding it out and dropping it on the ground. He did the same with the second bag but lowered it carefully onto the sand in case the camp stove inside made a noise.

Slipping out himself, he gently pushed the door closed until it clicked, then pushed it harder until it closed fully, the door flush with the body of the car. He peered around the windshield, but the watcher was still unaware of him. Reaching into his pocket, he removed the keys and glanced at the fob. The Land Cruiser was the same model as his hire car. It didn't have a physical key but an electronic key fob which unlocked the car once in the vehicle's proximity. He hoped it was set up the same as his, where the car locked and unlocked silently. But if it wasn't? John pondered for a moment, then put the keys back in his pocket.

Bending over, he slung a bag over each shoulder—damn, they were heavy. Looking toward Mansur, he could see him rising to his feet as if coming to help him, so he raised his hand, motioning for him to stay where he was. There was no point risking both their lives. It was then he noticed a fatal flaw in his plan—the trail of footsteps leading from Mansur's hiding place to the vehicle.

"Fuck, fuck, fuck." John cursed under his breath and grimaced. "Bugger it." He thought for a moment but couldn't think of a way to hide the trail. He had to hope the trail wouldn't be seen until they had put some distance between them—still, nothing he could do now. John closed his eyes, took a couple of deep breaths, then ran.

He reached the halfway distance, his legs burning, lungs heaving, and stopped. Mansur looked at him in concern and beckoned him over. John reached into his pocket, removed the keys, and pressed the lock button. Tensing his body, expecting a beep and a shout from the watcher on the dune, he looked back over his shoulder to see the Land Cruiser's lights blink on and off silently. Exhaling, he set off at a run toward Mansur.

So far, so good.

44

Taha shifted his weight, wriggling lower in the sand. Raising himself up onto his elbows, he unwound the *shemagh* from his neck and wiped the sweat from his face before wrapping it around his head. He glanced at his wristwatch and sighed. It had been three hours since he came to the top of the dune, and there was still no sign of the Englishman. Assuming he left at five for the sunrise at six and allowing another half an hour after the sunrise, he should have been back a long time ago. Taha would wait for another half an hour, then they would have to rethink their plan. He couldn't stay out in this heat. There was no shelter, and he had left the rest of the water in the car. Taha had learned the hard way in the *Légion* what heat and dehydration could do to a man. Picking up the binoculars, he scanned the horizon on all sides of the camp again. No sign of movement anywhere.

. . .

Down in the camp, Bogdan was also getting anxious. He checked his watch, then looked over at Adriana. She was lying on her front, her head turned away from him. His eyes roamed her body—her slim waist, the curve of her hips, her long tanned legs visible from thigh to ankle— he licked his lips and shifted his position as he felt his arousal growing. He would love to have a taste of her, but it was too risky right now. He had to be ready for the Englishman's arrival. Despite himself, he grinned—at least he wasn't lying in the sand like Taha. A sound outside caught his attention. He stiffened as he heard footsteps approaching along the path that led up to the tent. Picking up the PAMAS from his lap, he got slowly to his feet, and carefully placing each foot, made his way to the entrance of the tent. He stood with his back to the side of the tent and raised the weapon.

The footsteps came closer, and he closed his eyes, bringing all his focus on his hearing, straining to make out who the unseen intruder was. By the sound of the footsteps, it wasn't the Englishman, the footwear sounding soft and light. They stopped outside the door, then he heard the tinkle of the small brass bell which served as the doorbell for housekeeping. It definitely wasn't the Englishman; he wouldn't ring the bell. It must be the staff. Hopefully, they would go away if they didn't get a reply. He glanced over toward the bed as Adriana raised her head, her eyes wide with alarm. He pointed the gun at her and raised his left index finger to his lips, warning her to be silent.

The bell tinkled again. Bogdan turned the gun back toward the door and waited.

"Madam?"

Bogdan frowned. It was a woman's voice.

"Madam, okay?"

An accented woman's voice, not a native English speaker —Bogdan thought fast. It could be one of the other guests, but then they would use the woman's name. Then he remembered. The only other woman in the camp they had spotted during their recon the day before was a Bedouin woman. That explained the accent. It had to be her. He relaxed. She wouldn't come inside.

He turned back to face the bed and grinned at Adriana.

"Madam, you okay? I'm coming in."

Bogdan spun around and raised his weapon as Adriana cried out a muffled warning. He stepped forward, wrenched open the tent entrance and grabbed the woman, pulling her into the tent, throwing her on the ground. She rolled over and looked up at him, throwing her hands up in defense. Bogdan stood over her, pointing the gun at her head.

"Alzam alsamt," he commanded, using the little Arabic he knew. "Keep quiet."

Warda glared at him, then looked over at Adriana lying on the bed. Adriana looked back, her eyebrows creased together, her eyes watery with tears.

Bogdan reached into his cargo pants pocket with his left hand and pulled out a handful of cable ties. Stepping toward Warda, he kicked her in the side. She grunted in pain.

"Ibn al Kalb." She spat at his feet. "Son of a dog."

"Alzam alsamt, sharmuta," he growled back. "Keep quiet, bitch."

He placed his left boot on her wrist, pinning it to the ground, then knelt on his right knee and drilled the barrel of the gun into her temple, pushing her head to the side, facing away from him. Bogdan wished Taha was here to help him. With his left hand, he slipped a cable tie under the pinned wrist, slipped one end through the hole in the other, and ratcheted it tight. He slipped another cable tie through that one, then cursed. It wasn't easy with one hand. He pulled the gun away from her head and laid it on the floor behind him. Reaching down, he grabbed her other wrist. The woman struggled and pulled her hand free. Frustrated he slapped her on the side of the head, knelt on her chest, pinning her to the ground, and grabbed her hand again, pulling it toward him, then released her right wrist from under his boot, and pulled them both together. He wrapped the loose cable tie around her left wrist and pulled it tight, securing both wrists. Standing up, he caught his breath as she lay there, angry eyes drilling holes in him from behind her *niqab*. He would have preferred to secure her arms behind her back, but it was the best he could do by himself.

"Ayree feek," she cursed him, "Fuck you."

Bogdan shook his head. She would be a pain in the arse. He looked around for the duct tape and spotting it on the table, tore off a strip, bent down to remove the mask-like *niqab* that covered her face, and stuck the tape over her mouth. That would shut her up. He wasn't happy about her legs being unsecured, but he only had one cable tie left, and it wasn't long enough to go around both ankles. So, he pulled the hijab from her head, wound it into a rope, then sat on her legs and tied her ankles together.

Standing, he looked down at her, able for the first time to see her face. She wasn't bad looking, not a stunner like the woman on the bed but attractive, nonetheless. He estimated her age around thirty, her skin fair, protected from the ravages of the sun by her *niqab* and *hijab*, her hair raven black and long. When all this was over, he and Taha could definitely have some fun.

45

John lay on his back, gasping for air, his quadriceps and calves on fire with the lactic acid burn.

Mansur dragged the bags toward him and unzipping them, looked through the contents, then looked over at John.

"We have plenty of water now. Well done."

John pushed himself up on one elbow, swallowed, then reached into his pocket, pulled out the key fob, and held it up.

"I saw you do that. He won't be happy," Mansur grinned.

"Throw me the small pouches from the bags," John instructed. "I want to see who these guys are." He waited for Mansur to toss them over, then opened the first one and looked at the passport.

"Taha Kateb. Algerian. Twenty-seven years old," he read aloud, flicking through the pages. "Residence permit for the U.A.E." He picked up the other pouch and removed the passport.

"Hmm. Bogdan Kolisnick. Ukrainian. Thirty-five. He too has U.A.E residency." He frowned and looked up at Mansur.

"They're armed too. Steve was right. There's a box of rounds in the bag, 9mm, but at least we know there are only two of them."

"But what do they want from you, John? You're not a bad man."

"It's a long story, Mansur," John sighed and looked down at the sand, shaking his head. "The man who employed these... mercenaries, I assume... he took something from me a long time ago. Something... someone.... precious to me." John clenched his teeth. "I took my revenge."

"We have this here," Mansur nodded in understanding. "Not so much now, but in the old days. *Dum butlab dum.* How do you say? An eye for an eye? But John, it never ends. Not until everyone is dead."

"I know my friend, I know," John nodded and studied Mansur's face—a noble, honest face.

"Let's get this stuff back to the camels," John said, pushing himself to his feet. "We need to move fast." He pointed toward the Land Cruiser. "It's only a matter of time before he sees our footprints."

Mansur reached out and clasped John on the shoulder. *"Inshallah habibi*, we will fix this." He hoisted a bag onto the camel and made it secure.

John bent down, grabbed the strap of the other bag, and passed it over to Mansur. With a click of his tongue, Mansur instructed the camel to stand up, patting it gently on the neck. Turning to John, he said *"Yalla,"* and together, they headed back through the sand to where they left Steve and the other camels.

Twenty minutes later, they dropped the bags in the sand beside the camels and looked up at Steve at the top of the dune. Mansur gave a low whistle, and Steve's head whipped around. He raised a hand when he saw them and beckoned them up.

John looked at Mansur and shrugged. Unzipping the bag, he removed a bottle of water, and they climbed up the sandy slope. Dropping to his knees beside Steve, John handed him the bottle. Steve rolled onto his back, unscrewed the cap, took a sip, then wiped his mouth.

"There's a complication."

46

Taha adjusted the focus on his binoculars and watched for any sign of movement at the entrance to the tent. The Arab woman had gone inside five minutes before and had yet to come out. Taha assumed Bogdan had dealt with her. They couldn't afford to have anyone wandering around the camp, warning the others they were there. But like all plans, theirs was rapidly turning to shit. He sighed. It wasn't the first time. They had learned in the *Légion* nothing ever went as planned, but it didn't make things any easier. He scanned the surrounding dunes —still no sign of movement. It was now well past time the Englishman should have returned. Lowering the binoculars, he wiped the sweat from his face with the end of his *shemagh*. He needed to speak to Bogdan. They had to come up with another plan. He couldn't stay up here all day, it was too hot, and his water bottle was almost empty.

He slid down from the top of the dune and sat up. Unscrewing the cap of the plastic bottle, he drained the last of the tepid water, then threw the bottle away onto the sand. Wiping his lips, he stood up and made his way back down to the Land Cruiser. Approaching the driver's door, he reached out and pulled the handle—the door didn't move. Taha frowned and tried again. No luck. *Merde*! He was sure he had left it unlocked. He reached into the pocket of his cargos for the key fob. Not there. He tried the other pocket. His heartbeat started to rise, his eyebrows knitting together in concern. He tried the breast pockets of his shirt. Empty.

"Enculer!" he cursed. "Fuck!"

He patted himself down again, but apart from a spare magazine, his pockets were empty. Turning, he looked back up the face of the dune. It must have fallen out while he was lying in the sand. He shook his head and set off back up the dune, studying his footprints for any sign of the key fob. Reaching the top, he dropped to his knees and scanned the area, but couldn't see anything. He dug his hands in the sand, letting it run through his fingers until he had dug through the whole area, about two square meters—nothing. Now, he started to panic. The day was just going from bad to worse, and he wasn't looking forward to telling Bogdan he'd lost the keys. He thought fast, visualizing his movements over the past couple of hours. When he had driven the vehicle over, he had parked, then walked to the back, opened the tailgate, and removed a bottle of water before climbing the dune face. The key must have fallen out then.

He pushed himself up, then trudged back down the sand to the vehicle. Starting at the driver's door, he walked slowly to the rear, scanning the ground for the keys—nothing. He lowered himself to the ground and looked under the car in the unlikely event they had bounced underneath—again, nothing. Standing, he brushed the sand off his front and stood with his hands on his hips. He didn't remember walking around the other side of the car, but he'd better check. He was getting desperate now. All their water, travel documents, clothing, money, and extra ammunition were in the vehicle. Without the keys, they were screwed. He walked around the back, praying for a glimpse of a black key fob lying in the sand. Rounding the corner of the vehicle, he stopped. Beside the front passenger door, something had disturbed the sand, and a trail of footprints led away from the vehicle.

"Fils de pute!" He reached behind him and removed his weapon. "Son of a bitch!" Cocking it, he started to follow the trail of footprints, one eye on the trail, one ahead, searching for activity in the dunes. After about fifty meters, he stopped and looked down. The sand here was also disturbed. He crouched and examined the tracks. It looked like two men had laid in the sand. Standing, he looked around. Two sets of footprints led to and from the flattened area—two men. He paused and looked closer—something else, the unmistakable two-toed shape of a camel's footprints. Taha's grip tightened on his handgun.

"Fucking thieving Arabs!"

Taha walked on a little way and scanned the horizon ahead. He could see where the tracks disappeared among the dunes but had no clue how far away the thieves were. He looked up at the sun and cursed. Checking his watch, he did a quick calculation. He'd been keeping a lookout on the dune for almost four hours. They could be miles away by now. He had used up his water, and the day was only getting hotter. It would be foolish to follow them. He was a fit, battle-hardened man, but without water, there was no way he could track them down, let alone keep up with them on foot. With a camel, they could make twice the speed he could. He banged his left fist against his thigh in frustration.

"Merde, merde, merde!" he cursed, making no effort to keep his voice down. He slid the PAMAS back into his waist-

band and turning, trudged back through the sand to the Land Cruiser. Cupping his hands around his face, he peered through the glass, but the tint, while welcome when inside the vehicle, prevented him from seeing in. Taha bit his lip. They could always commandeer another vehicle, but they needed their passports and wallets if they hoped to get out of the country safely.

He removed the PAMAS from his belt, double checked the safety was on, then gripping it by the barrel, swung it in an arc toward the window. Nothing happened the first time, so he swung it again, and the glass cracked. Once more, he swung, and fine lines spread out across the glass like a spiderweb, the tinted window film holding the glass together and preventing it from shattering. He returned the weapon to his waistband, then using his elbow, struck the window a couple more times until the glass fell inside the vehicle. Reaching inside, he unlocked the door, opening it wide.

On the floor between the seats was a pile of clothes. He looked over the rear seat into the trunk and saw both their bags were missing, as was some of their camping equipment. Taha cursed again and sorted through the clothes, hoping his passport had been left behind. Shit! No passport, no money, no spare ammunition, and all the water was gone. He climbed out of the car and slammed the door shut. He had to get back to the camp and break the news to Bogdan.

47

"You said your tent is the one closest to us on the right?" Steve pointed. "That one?"

"Yes," affirmed John.

"About ten minutes ago, I saw a woman enter the tent and not come out. She was dressed like a local, didn't look like a guest."

"Warda," Mansur sucked in a breath. "What was she wearing?"

"I couldn't see clearly at this distance, but it looked like she was wearing a light blue *hijab* and looked like something covered her face."

Mansur muttered something unintelligible in Arabic.

John turned to Mansur. "Your wife is the only woman in the camp?"

"Yes."

"Shit."

The three men lay there in silence, staring out across the sand toward the tented camp.

"I'm sorry. It's my fault they're here." John looked over to his right at Mansur. "It's me they want. I'm sorry I've dragged you into this."

Mansur glanced over at John, his eyes moist, then went back to staring at the camp as if willing Warda out of the tent.

John rolled over onto his back and looked up at the sky. Closing his eyes, he felt the heat of the sun burning into his skin. Why was his life so cursed? Why was any chance of happiness torn away from him? He thought his luck had changed when he met Adriana. Maybe he just wasn't meant to be happy?

He opened his eyes at a sound from Mansur and rolled over to look back at the camp.

"Habibi," whispered Mansur as they watched the two small figures of his daughters running between the tents. A tear rolled down from the corner of his eye.

John gritted his teeth. He had to do something, and he had to do it fast.

"Look," Steve whispered. Away to the left, a man emerged on foot from behind the dunes and made his way toward the tents.

Mansur narrowed his eyes. "That's the lookout."

"Shit. He must have discovered we robbed the Land Cruiser." John looked at Steve and explained, "He left his keys, so I took them and locked the vehicle. I was hoping we would have more time before he found out." John sighed, rubbing his face.

"Guys, we have to change our plan. We can't wait them out now. It's too risky. It won't be long before the staff realizes Warda is missing, and Adriana and I haven't been seen." He nodded in the camp's direction. "I don't want those kids to be harmed. We have to go down there."

"John, there is no way we can approach the camp

without being spotted. It will be suicide. Why don't we just go to the police?"

"No, Steve," Mansur shook his head. "It will take an hour minimum before we can get to somewhere with a cell phone signal. Maybe another two hours before the police come. It's too long."

"Mansur's right, Steve. I'm not waiting that long. It's too risky."

"Then what do we do?"

John pursed his lips, an idea starting to form in the back of his brain. It would be risky, but he couldn't think of anything else.

48

Taha lay in a depression in the sand, not moving, his eyes on the camp ahead. The kitchen staff moved back-and-forth from the dining tent to the kitchen building, clearing away the remains of breakfast.

There was no movement from the reception building, and outside one of the tents, a tall, thin European man sat in a chair, writing in a journal.

Taha ignored him since he was facing in the opposite direction. Instead, he concentrated on the camp staff. No-one should see him approaching the tent. So far, apart from the Arab woman, no-one knew they were there, and he intended to keep it that way.

Five minutes passed. Taha kept low, waiting, not moving. Then when all the staff had disappeared, he raised himself off the ground and staying low and keeping the tent between him and the staff area, he sprinted across the sand. Reaching the tent, he stopped, bent double as he regained his breath

"Bogdan. I'm coming in," he hissed.

"Oui," came the reply from inside.

Taha opened the door and stepped in. It took a moment for his eyes to adjust to the darkness after the glare outside, and he used the time to bring his breathing back to normal. Bogdan sat on a chair in the corner, the PAMAS lying in his lap. On the floor lay the Arab woman, her legs bound with a light blue cloth, her hands secured in front of her, a strip of tape across her mouth. The dim light failed to hide the venom pouring from her eyes. On the bed, propped up against the headboard sat the foreign woman, similarly bound. She too glared at him.

"Why did you come back?" Bogdan questioned.

Taha sighed. There was no easy way to say this. Turning to Bogdan and keeping his voice low, he filled him in.

"Someone broke into the Land Cruiser. They've stolen all our supplies, passports, and money."

"Fils de pute!" Bogdan cursed, jumping to his feet, catching the PAMAS before it slipped off his lap. *"Comment?"*

Taha shrugged and raised his hands in that typical Gallic way, at the same time pulling down his mouth.

"I had left it unlocked. There was no-one around. How could I know?"

"Enculer!" Bogdan cursed again as he paced back-and-forth. He stopped and faced Taha. "Do you think...?"

"The Englishman? *C'est possible, mais non,* I don't think so."

"Pourqouis? Why?"

"Camel tracks. I think it was locals."

Bogdan nodded slowly, his face fixed in a scowl. He looked at the two women. A thought struck him.

"Parlez vous Francais?" he addressed Adriana.

There was no sign of comprehension on her face, just a frown.

"Do you speak French?"

She shook her head.

Good, thought Bogdan. The Arab woman wouldn't understand either.

"If it was locals, why didn't they take the car?" he asked Taha, continuing in French.

"I don't know. Maybe it's too hard. Food, water, money? Easier to hide."

"Hmmm," Bogdan wasn't convinced.

"If it was the Englishman, why didn't he take the car?"

Bogdan didn't reply. It wasn't worth wasting time on the why. They had to think of what to do now. He exhaled loudly. Their plan had really turned to shit.

49

Adriana listened with interest, happy she had the presence of mind to feign a lack of comprehension of French. These men were typical in their underestimation of women.

Her initial fear and concern had worn off as time passed. Now, she was more focused on getting free. The travel alarm clock she kept by the side of the bed had shown how much time had passed since the men first entered the tent, and as the hours passed, she became more confident John was aware the men were here. At first, she had felt terror—a little for herself but more about losing John. These men were armed and looked hard, especially the European. The younger North African-looking man seemed to defer to him. But why did they speak French? Maybe they were French. There were plenty of North Africans in France, although the European looked more like he was from Eastern Europe. John had never mentioned anything to do with France, so why were French speakers after him? Nothing made sense.

Her feelings for John had grown since their time in

Thailand, their shared travel over the past month had only brought them closer. She didn't want to lose him. As the men discussed the theft from the Land Cruiser, she knew deep down John was behind it.

John was a kind, loving man, calm and generous, but somewhere inside, he had a core of steel. She had glimpsed that in Thailand during the events involving Hassan and the traffickers. Something in his life had made him that way. She didn't know what, he still hadn't told her, but it would have been something bad. That explained the occasional nightmares and the times she had found him staring into the distance, sadness etched into his face. She had been reluctant to probe, assuming he would tell her when the time was right.

Seeing the consternation on the French-speaking men's faces, she was now more confident than ever he would come to her rescue. She had to believe it. There was no point in sitting in despair.

Adriana could just see Warda's head on the floor and from the determined glare from her eyes, she knew she hadn't given up either and would fight when the time was right. But how to get free, and what could she do when she did so?

A thought struck her, and she grunted as loud as the duct tape would allow. The two men stopped talking and looked at her. She jerked her head toward the toilet door. The European one shook his head and went back to talking to the North African-looking man. She groaned louder and lifted her feet and banged them up and down on the mattress.

The European sighed and spoke to his colleague. "Take her to the toilet, but don't untie her."

"But...?"

"Just do it. You've fucked up already today."

The North African nodded, walked over to the bed, and moving Adriana's legs to the side, pulled her toward him until her feet were touching the floor. Her nightdress rode up, exposing a pair of black silk knickers, and he averted his eyes while the European looked on with a grin. The man grabbed her by the arm and pulled her up to a standing position, the hem of her nightdress slipping down again to cover her legs. Keeping hold of her arm, he steadied her as she hopped toward the toilet, the door of which he opened with his left hand. Guiding her through, he pushed her toward the w/c and stood back. Adriana looked at him and raised her shoulders in a shrug. He sighed, then stepped forward, knelt before her, and closing his eyes, reached up underneath her nightdress and pulled her panties down to her knees. He stood up, opened his eyes, and said, *"Pardon."*

Adriana nodded. Placing his hands on her shoulders, he pushed her down on the toilet seat, then turned and walked away, stepping out from the toilet.

Adriana breathed a sigh of relief—she needed him to be outside for what she had in mind. She tensed as she heard the two men talking in French outside, one protesting the other had come out, the North African explaining he wouldn't watch her, and she couldn't go anywhere. His argument won the day. The discussion stopped, and the man remained outside.

As quickly and quietly as she could, she stood up and shuffled across to the small vanity unit. On top was John's toilet kit, fortunately unzipped after he had used it earlier that morning. She remembered he carried a small Swiss Army knife inside. Turning her back on it, she probed behind her with the fingers of her bound hands until she grasped the pouch. Slowly, she pulled it toward her, then put her fingers inside and felt around, sorting through the items inside until she felt what seemed to be the knife. She ran her fingers along each side until she was confident it was the right thing, then removed it. Carefully, she pushed the pouch back to where it had been, then turned around. She didn't think the North African would notice anything, he hadn't been in the room long enough. She cupped the pocketknife in her hands, covering it from view, then moved back to the toilet and sat down. Fortunately, she did have to pee, just in case they got suspicious.

Finishing, she stood up and made a noise. The door opened, and the man looked inside. She nodded, and he came forward, once again closing his eyes as he pulled her panties up. Taking her by the arm, he led her out the door and back to the bed. Sitting down, she slid back against the headrest, the knife safely hidden from sight.

50

The three men gathered at the foot of the dune.

"I have an idea," explained John. "Steve, can you tell us anything else about these guys? We need to know who we're dealing with."

"I know as much as you, mate. Until yesterday, I had never seen them before."

John walked over to the pack camel and unzipped one of the bags he had taken from the Land Cruiser. He pulled out the travel pouches and tossed them over to Steve, who caught one but missed the other which fell at his feet.

"Look at those," John instructed. "See if you can spot anything I've missed."

Steve opened the first and looked inside. Removing the passport, he scanned through the information page, making a face.

"North African." He flipped through the pages. "A lot of stamps—Iraq, Sudan, Congo, ah, a Dubai residence permit." He looked up at John. "Could be a mercenary or a security contractor. The countries he's been to, not the first places I would choose for tourism." He pulled out the wallet. "Dubai driving license, credit cards—nothing out of the ordinary." He rezipped the travel pouch and tossed it back to John. Bending down, he picked up the other one and repeated the process.

"Ukrainian, similar stamps to the first one." He shrugged. "I would say ex-military of some sort, now working privately." He pulled out the wallet, flipped through it, and pulled out a business card. "Here we go. *Frontiere Oriental Moyen*. I've heard of them. Supposed to be private security for traveling executives, but I've heard rumors. Hired guns."

"Shit. Well, it can't be helped." John made a face and rubbed his eyes. "Now we know they're obviously trained *and* armed." He looked from Steve to Mansur and back again. "Look, I can't sit back and do nothing. It will take too long for anyone to get here. I have to do something. You guys stay here. It's because of me they're here. I don't want you to get hurt."

"I'm coming with you, John," replied Mansur. "My *habibi* is also there. No man will ever harm my wife and get away with it."

"Okay."

Steve watched them both, chewing on his lip.

"John, before we go any further, I want to know what these men want from you. Why is Surya Patil hell-bent on finding you and sending these men after you? If I'm going to help you, I need to know."

John narrowed his eyes. Why should he tell him? He hadn't even told Adriana. But the three of them together would have more chance of overpowering the two mercenaries. He glanced toward Mansur, who gave an almost imperceptible nod. John sighed and fixed Steve in his gaze. Steve stood patiently, waiting for an answer.

"Surya Patil's son raped and murdered my wife."

"Shit, mate. I'm sorry," Steve sighed. "That sucks." He frowned, "But why is he after you now?"

John paused, looked up at the sky, said nothing for a while, then looked back at Steve.

"Because I took my revenge. An eye for an eye."

"Fuck! Really?" Steve blew air out through his pursed lips and shook his head. "Man, no wonder he's after you." He shook his head again. "Shit." Steve glanced at Mansur, who was watching him, studying his reactions. He turned back to John. "This was in India?"

John nodded.

"You know what that man said? The skinny one? They made a movie about him?"

John frowned, not sure what Steve was referring to.

"Anyway, he said 'an eye for an eye will make the whole world blind.'"

"So, what are you saying? I should have let him get away with it? Stood by and done nothing? Surya Patil is a powerful man. Powerful men in India are untouchable. It's not Australia, Steve." John shrugged. "Anyway, I don't expect you to understand. I did what I had to, and I'll do what I have to now."

"No mate,"—Steve raised his hands—"I understand. I was a cop. The system, even in Australia, doesn't always work as it should. Mate, in your position, I would probably have done the same. In fact, the amount I have to keep paying my ex-wife, maybe..." He gave a half smile, then frowned again. "Look, mate, all I'm saying is these things never end. That skinny bugger..."

"Gandhi."

"Yeah, him. He was right. The whole world will go blind."

"No, I will end it."

"Yeah,"—Steve nodded slowly—"you'll have to." He stepped forward and clasped John on the shoulder. "I'm with you, mate. Let's get these bastards, then we'll have a couple of cold ones. I'm gasping."

"Cold ones?" Mansur looked puzzled.

"Beers mate. Beers."

51

"I assume these two men have seen your vehicle, Steve?"

"Yup."

"Hmm, okay." John nodded. "It's a risk we have to take because we can't approach on foot. But Pajeros are pretty common."

"What's your idea?"

"We take your Pajero. They know what we look like so you and I will hide in the back. Mansur, you drive. The chances are they haven't seen you, and it will look like you've come to pick someone up or make a delivery."

"Yes, most of the tourists have a local driver."

"Exactly," John agreed. "And most of the hire cars are white SUV's, so I think they won't recognize Steve's car. To be sure we can remove the plates."

Both men nodded.

"So, Mansur. You drive up to the camp and park in a way the rear doors can't be seen. You go into the reception, then Steve and I'll slip out the back of the car. Got it?"

"Yes."

"Is there a secure place where we can put the other guests and the staff?"

Mansur thought. "Not really."

"How many staff are there?"

Mansur did a mental calculation, his lips moving silently as he went through the names.

"There are three kitchen and housekeeping staff—Fouad, Umar, Razak, and Thomas at the reception."

"The Indian guy?"

"Yes, so four… and my daughters."

"Okay, six plus the German couple and the other English couple. Ten people."

"Don't forget the other two drivers. The guests came with drivers."

"Ah yes, so twelve." John thought for a moment, then looked at his watch. "The other guests will probably check out soon. Mansur, how long do people stay for?"

"No-one ever stays for more than one night. It's too hot during the day."

"Good. What time do they normally leave?"

"Anywhere from ten-thirty onward."

"So, the chances are they will leave anytime now. That'll be six less to worry about. Just leaves the four staff and your daughters, Mansur. That's better. We need to get them as far from my tent as possible. Even if we put them in the kitchen building, they will be safer. Can it be locked from the inside?"

"Yes."

"What about the windows?"

"They have shutters to keep the sand out. We can close them."

"Good. That sounds okay."

"So, we wait until they leave before going in?" asked Steve.

"Yes. I don't want to risk anyone's life. It will be hard enough protecting Adriana and Warda without adding more people."

"It makes sense, John," replied Mansur. "Then what do we do? We can't just walk into the tent."

"No, we need to draw them out somehow. I haven't thought that far ahead yet," he sighed.

"Look, mate, we can't plan for everything. Let's get in there and make sure the others are safe first."

John looked at Steve. "Yes, one step at a time." He looked at Mansur, then back at Steve. "It's not too late to say no. You don't have to come with me. I'll go whatever happens."

"I'm with you, mate. I've not had this much excitement for a long time."

"I'm coming too, my friend," agreed Mansur.

John nodded, then smiled. "Thank you. Right, let's do it."

52

Gunther looked up from his journal as the two young Bedouin girls walked past his tent, holding hands. He smiled and raised his hand in greeting, "Good morning."

The girls stopped, and the older of the two gave him a dull stare but said nothing. He glanced down at the smaller one, her eyes red and puffy, a trail of mucus running from her nose.

"What's the matter?"

"*Umi, Abu?*" the older one asked while the younger one sniffed and wiped her cheek.

"Your mother, your father?" Gunther was puzzled. Standing, he gave his biggest grandfatherly smile. "Come, I will take you to them." Johanna was still packing. They had been married for almost fifty years and had traveled the world together, yet she still took forever to pack. Despite only staying the one night, she had somehow filled the tent with her belongings, in contrast to his already packed and tidy suitcase, but he had learned from experience to let her get on with it. Stepping onto the sand, he beckoned the girls to follow him and led them along the path to the reception building, the youngest girl still sniffling and weeping.

Gunther walked into the open plan reception area and smiled at the young Indian man sitting at the desk. On one of the long seats lining one wall sat Gunther's driver, Tariq, who stood as he entered.

"Good morning, Sir. Are you ready to go?"

"Good morning, Tariq. We'll be with you soon." Turning to the Indian man, he looked at his name tag and said, "Thomas, these two girls are looking for their mother and father."

Thomas stood up and looked over the counter at the two girls.

"Yes, Sir. Mansur and Warda." He frowned. "Actually, I haven't seen Mansur this morning, but their mother was here before breakfast."

Gunther reached into the bowl on the reception counter and removed two candies, passing them to the girls, who accepted without a word, then turned back to Thomas.

"Can I leave them with you, young man?"

"Yes, of course," Thomas smiled. "I'll take them to their mother."

Tariq, the driver, spoke in Arabic, addressing the two girls. The eldest girl answered. He spoke again, then switched to English for the benefit of Gunther and Thomas.

"She said she hasn't seen her father since last night."

Thomas frowned. "That's unusual." He came around the desk and glanced out the window. "His camels aren't here either." He squatted down and looked at the girls. "Ask them if their father said where he was going?"

Tariq asked in Arabic. "She says her mother told her he was going out in the desert for the sunrise."

"Ah, that's okay." Thomas smiled and stood up. "He does

that sometimes, although..." He checked his watch, "He's normally back by now." He smiled at Gunther. "Don't worry, Sir, I'll look after them. I'll take them to their mother. Farida, Saara, *yalla*." He smiled at the girls, leading them out the door toward the staff building.

Gunther turned to Tariq. "Thank you, Tariq. My wife is just finishing her packing."

"Yes, Sir. Please take your time."

"Thank you."

Gunther stepped out and walked back toward his tent. Come to think of it, he hadn't seen the nice young couple this morning, John and... Adriana. The other guests, the unfriendly English couple, had been at breakfast the same time as he and Johanna and departed the camp thirty minutes earlier without a word or a glance in his direction. He didn't think John and Adriana would be that unfriendly.

He reached his tent and opening the door, looked inside. He shook his head. "Johanna, *meine liebchen*, are you ready?" he asked, although the answer was obvious. It still looked like a whirlwind had passed through.

"*Nein*. Five minutes."

"Okay," Gunther chuckled. She had said that fifteen minutes ago. He would leave her to it. Closing the door, he looked toward the last tent. He would go and say goodbye to John and Adriana.

53

It took only twenty minutes to get back to the Pajero. Riding the camels, with Mansur urging them on, they kept a rapid pace. Once dismounted, Mansur hobbled the camels, so they wouldn't wander far, then removed a collapsible bowl made from goatskin and filled it with water from the water bottles raided from the Land Cruiser. One by one, he made sure the camels had water while John and Steve removed the number plates, using a screwdriver from the toolbox found in the rear of the Pajero. With a pat on the neck and a kind word for each of the camels, Mansur walked over to where John and Steve were squatting in the shade of the Pajero, the number plates in the sand beside them. The heat was stifling, even in the shade. John passed one of the remaining bottles to Mansur, and the three men sipped the water, ensuring they were hydrated.

"Will they be okay?" John asked.

Mansur looked back at the camels. "Yes. *Inshallah,* we won't be away too long. They can survive in this heat, unlike us."

"All being well." John patted him on the shoulder. "We'll be back for them later today, my friend."

Mansur nodded silently, concern for his animals evident on his face.

John stood up. "Let's go."

Steve stood, removed the Pajero keys from his pocket, and handed them to Mansur, who opened the driver's door and climbed in. Steve walked around the back and opened the rear load hatch and climbed in, John closing it behind him before he opened the rear passenger door and sat in the rear seat.

"*Yalla,* let's go."

Mansur drove with skill, instinctively knowing where to find traction, years of living and driving in the desert, giving him an innate knowledge of the sand and how to navigate. John stared out the front window, trying to imagine what would happen when they reached the camp, running through different scenarios in his mind while Steve braced himself in the trunk as the vehicle pitched and rolled like a ship on the sea. They made good progress and took less than a third of the time it had taken them on the camels earlier that morning.

Rather than take them straight back the way they had come, Mansur took a circuitous route and rejoined the main track a little North of the camp to make it look like he was coming from Bidiyah. In the distance, a dust cloud thrown up by a white vehicle heading in the opposite direction signaled a departing guest.

"Good, that's one lot of guests away safely. I wonder if that was the Germans or the other couple."

"I don't know, but we'll reach the camp soon," replied Mansur. "Better you hide now."

John ducked down and curled himself up on the floor

between the front and rear seats while Steve laid himself flat in the back.

Mansur swerved too late to miss a bump in the track, and the Pajero wallowed and bounced, bringing a string of colourful curses from the rear.

"Sorry," apologized Mansur through gritted teeth, his eyes scanning the road surface for further hazards.

John felt the vehicle slowing, then Mansur confirmed their arrival.

"We are here."

"Take it slowly. Any sign of them?"

Mansur scanned the camp as he slowed down and entered the parking at a crawl.

"No. There is still one vehicle here, so one of the guests hasn't left yet." He swung the wheel over and parked at an angle behind the reception building, keeping the building between the vehicle and the tents. "It's the German couple. I can see their driver waiting in the reception."

"Damn," muttered John. He liked them and didn't want them to be in harm's way. He exhaled slowly, calming his nerves. "Which side should we get out?"

"The right but wait. I'll check the reception and make sure it's safe, then I'll come back as if I've forgotten something."

"Okay."

Mansur opened the door and stepped out, and John and Steve waited, the only sound the ticking and creaking of the cooling engine.

A minute later, Mansur came back and opened the door, leaning in as if getting something from the glove compartment.

"All clear," he whispered.

54

Gunther walked slowly down the path toward the last tent. He gazed around at the surrounding dunes and marveled at the beauty of the landscape, the colors of the sand, the undulations of the dunes rising and falling around them. He loved the country and the desert, but the heat, although a pleasant change from the German winter, made it a difficult place to spend a lot of time. He was looking forward to their next stop. By evening, he and Johanna would be high up in the cool air of the Omani mountains, a complete contrast to where they were now. That's if his wife finished packing. He chuckled to himself as he neared John's tent.

He heard muffled voices from inside. It sounded like two men talking. He shrugged; he must be mistaken. His hearing wasn't what it used to be. Reaching up, he rang the little brass bell that hung from the awning.

He waited and looked around. Over by the kitchen block, he could see Thomas talking to the other staff, the little figures of the two young girls beside him. The sound of an approaching vehicle caught his ear, and he glanced toward the parking area as a white SUV pulled in behind the reception building and disappeared. Turning back to the tent, he frowned. He was sure he'd heard voices inside, but no-one had responded to the bell. He rang it again, then called out,

"Adriana, John. It is Gunther. I came to say goodbye." There was the sound of movement from inside. "Hello?" he called out again. "Is everything okay?" Gunther heard a throat being cleared, then a woman's voice.

"Yes, Gunther, good morning."

"Good morning, Adriana. Is everything okay? Johanna and I didn't see you at breakfast."

There was a pause, then, "Everything is okay. My stomach was upset, so I stayed in bed."

"Oh, no. Is there anything I can do?"

"No, it's okay. Thank you... I'm sorry I can't come out."

Gunther frowned again. "It's okay. You rest. Is John there? I haven't seen him either?"

"He's... in the bathroom."

Gunther nodded, forgetting she couldn't see him.

"That's a pity. Please tell him I said goodbye. It was a pleasure meeting you both."

Another pause. "You too. Have a safe journey... Be careful."

He heard a noise but was convinced his ears were playing tricks on him. He must go for another checkup after the holiday.

"Auf wiedersen," he called out, but there was no reply.

Shrugging, he turned and started making his way back to his tent. The conversation was strange, stilted, unlike the friendly conversation of the night before. Something seemed off this morning. Maybe they'd fought? He'd had his share of arguments with Johanna over the years; no couple was immune. Or perhaps it was because she was unwell. Oh well, the least he could do was let the staff know she wasn't well. The camp must have access to a doctor or medicines. He passed his tent and headed back toward reception. He hoped she would get better soon, but it was strange that no-one had seen John either.

55

Taha stood inside the tent, his ear to the door, listening to the sound of Gunther walking away. Once the sound had faded, he nodded at Bogdan who was standing beside the bed, the barrel of his automatic pressing into the side of Adriana's head. He pulled it away, switched hands, then slapped her across the face. The duct tape, now stuck back over her mouth, muffled her gasp as she fell sideways across the bed.

"Stupid bitch! I warned you," Bogdan growled.

"It's okay," Taha frowned. "He's gone."

Bogdan shook his head angrily. "We have to be careful. The job's not finished yet." He looked at his watch. "This guy should have been back by now. Something's wrong."

Taha nodded and put his weapon away. "What do we do? We can't stay here."

"No." Bogdan walked closer, turned, and looked down at the Arab woman on the floor, then back at Adriana on the bed. "We need to replace the vehicle first. We should be ready when he comes back."

"What about the passports?"

"We can drive across the border at an unmanned point and get replacements when we are back in Dubai. That's not the problem. The problem is now someone out there has proof we've been here." Bogdan rubbed his face then turned and kicked the leg of the bed. *"Merde!"*

Taha watched and said nothing.

"We'll have to worry about that later. First, we finish the job, or we don't get paid, and this will have been for nothing. One thing's for fucking sure. I'm asking for a bonus once we're done."

"There are two vehicles up by the reception; we can take one of those," Taha suggested. "But the staff will see us. We'll have lost the element of surprise."

"Forget surprise. This guy hasn't come back yet. I think he knows."

"How can he know?"

"I don't know, but something's not right. Think about our Land Cruiser. It's a bit of a coincidence our gear was stolen."

"Locals."

"Have you seen any locals out here? We're miles from anywhere. No, I'm sure it was him. He's smarter than we think." Bogdan looked back at Adriana, who had sat back up and was watching them with ill-disguised fury. "But we still have the advantage. We have his woman."

"Oui."

"D'accord. Let's gain some control again. We need a vehicle, and we need to get out of this fucking tent."

56

John slipped out of the Pajero, followed by Steve. Keeping to a crouch, they crept around the back and into reception, keeping low and away from the open door and window spaces. Thomas was nowhere to be seen, just a bewildered looking Omani, who John assumed to be one of the drivers.

"Who are you?"

"I am Tariq, Sir," he replied. Turning to Mansur, he asked in Arabic, "What's going on?"

"You are driving for the Germans?" John interrupted,

"Yes, Mr. Gunther and his wife." Tariq looked back-and-forth between the three men, clearly perplexed.

"Tariq, we need your help. It's very important you listen carefully."

"What's happening?"

Mansur explained, switching to Arabic, Tariq's expression changing from perplexed to shock. He nodded, then asked in English, "What can I do?"

"The first thing we need to do is to get your guests to safety. Are they ready to leave?"

"I think so. Mr. Gunther was here a moment ago."

"Okay," John nodded thoughtfully. "Tariq, these men know who I am." He pointed to Steve. "They know who he is. We can't go. Can you find them and explain they have to leave immediately? But do it without alerting the men in my tent?"

"Yes, *Inshallah.*"

"Good. Get them out of here as fast as you can. As soon as you get to Bidiyah, I want you to contact the police. Tell them we have a hostage situation. Tell them two men have raided the camp and taken guests hostage. Can you do that?"

"Yes, of course."

"Good, go now."

Tariq walked toward the doorway, looked down the pathway, stopped, and turned.

"Mr. Gunther is coming this way now. What should I do?"

"Wait, let him come here."

A moment later, Gunther stepped inside and looked around. His eyes lit up, and he smiled when he saw John.

"John, I've been looking for you. I thought something might be wrong, you didn't come to breakfast... Adriana said you were in the toilet..." He trailed off when he saw John's expression. "What's the matter?"

"Gunther, please move away from the doorway. Come over here and sit down."

Gunther complied, looking from John to Tariq, then at Steve. John guided him to the seating and sat down beside him.

"Gunther, some men have come to the camp. I believe they are in my tent and have taken Adriana hostage."

Realization crossed Gunther's face, and he nodded slowly. "*Ja*, that explains it."

"What do you mean?"

"I went to your tent to say goodbye. I hadn't seen either of you. Adriana answered from inside." Gunther paused and looked at the other men.

"Go on. What did she say?"

"She said she had been unwell and was resting. She didn't come out, and I thought it was because she was sick, but..."

"But what?"

"I thought I heard other voices, male voices... but then I thought maybe I was imagining things."

"You were right. There are men in there." John placed his hand on Gunther's arm. "We'll deal with it, but first, we'll get you and Johanna to safety."

"Johanna is still in our tent. I have to get her."

"No, Gunther, wait here. I don't want you to get hurt."

"But Johanna?"

John gave Gunther's shoulder a reassuring pat, then turned to Tariq. "Can you do it?"

"Yes."

"Good. As quick as you can but try not to frighten her."

"Wait," Gunther spoke up. "John, Tariq, I appreciate what you're doing, but she will be frightened." He stood and straightened, squaring his jaw. "I need to go with Tariq."

John frowned and rose to his feet.

"Gunther, these men are dangerous. We believe they're armed. It's too risky."

"John, we've been married for almost fifty years. She means everything to me," Gunther smiled. "Do you really think I will leave her there? I will go. She will trust me."

Without waiting for an answer, he walked across the

reception and stepped out the door. Tariq glanced at John and Mansur, then rushed out after him. John looked questioningly at Steve, who shrugged.

John didn't like it, but Gunther had a point. It was better a familiar face went to get her, so she didn't panic.

"Mansur, find your daughters and make sure the staff is safe. Barricade them in the kitchen block. The last thing we want is the boys going down to clean the rooms and getting caught. But be careful."

"Those men don't know who I am. I'm just another Arab to them."

John squeezed Mansur's arm. "Good luck. Once they're safe, come back here."

Mansur nodded and stepped out the door.

John turned to look at Steve and let out a long breath.

"What do we do next, mate?"

"I have no idea, Steve. I have no idea."

57

Taha stepped out the door onto the sandy path and hesitated. He saw a movement at the front of the next tent and stepped back, pulling the door closed.

"What is it?" Bogdan asked from inside the tent.

Taha said nothing but held up a hand, signaling for him to be quiet. He watched as the old man and his wife in the neighboring tent stepped out, followed by their driver, pulling their suitcases behind him. They turned and walked up to the path toward the reception.

Taha turned back and looked at Bogdan, "The old couple from the next tent are leaving. Should I go?"

"No, wait. That leaves just the staff for us to worry about. Makes it easier."

"But they will take their vehicle."

"It doesn't matter. There's the Englishman's vehicle and the old pickup the camp uses. We'll take one, then dump it in Bidiyah and steal something else. Better to wait. We still need to get away without getting caught."

Taha continued to watch through the crack in the door

as the couple and their driver disappeared inside the reception building. A moment later, the driver was just visible, opening the rear of their Land Cruiser and loading the bags into the vehicle.

The sound of the engine carried toward him, and he watched the old man walk around behind the vehicle and climb in, joining his wife on the rear passenger seat. The door closed, and the vehicle backed out, then with a brief toot of the horn, turned and sped off down the track.

"They've gone."

"*Bon.* Get us a vehicle. *Allez!*"

Taha opened the door once more and stepped out. Closing the door behind him, he looked around. The camp was quiet now, the guests having departed. The door to the kitchen block was closed, and the staff was nowhere to be seen. So far, so good. He sprinted across the gap between the two tents toward the reception, then paused, looking first at the reception block, then the kitchen building. He heard voices from the kitchen block, but the reception building seemed quiet—all the better. Hopefully, the keys to one of the vehicles would be kept there.

He took a breath and ran across, between the next two tents—still no sign of anyone. It looked like, finally, their luck was changing. With a glance around the edge of the tent, toward the kitchen, he took another breath, then sprinted the remaining fifty meters to the reception. Slowing, he leaped up the low step and entered the reception building. There was no-one behind the desk. Good. He heard a noise and looked to his right—just in time to see a fist heading for his face.

58

The man leaping through the door caught John by surprise. Steve was quicker, stepping forward and piling a hard right cross into the man's jaw. The man fell sideways, blood and spit flying from his mouth. By the time he hit the floor, John had regained his senses and leaped forward, swinging his right foot into the man's side. The man cried out and tried to scramble away. John kicked him again, this time, hearing a satisfying crunch as one of his ribs gave way. Jumping on top, he flipped him over and sat on his back, pinning his arms to the ground with his knees. He grabbed the man's hair and pulled his head back before smashing his face into the concrete floor again and again until the man gave up struggling.

John panted, adrenaline coursing through his body, flinching when he felt Steve's hand on his shoulder.

"He's tenderized, mate."

"Check for a weapon."

"I think you're sitting on it."

John felt the hard shape of a gun underneath him and shifted his position, reaching behind him to remove the weapon from the man's waistband. He handed it to Steve, who took a quick look, cocked it, and pointed it at the man's head.

"You can get off him now."

John got to his feet, walked behind the man, grabbed his feet, and dragged him away from the doorway before turning him over. The man opened his eyes, still groggy, his face a mass of bloody and bruised flesh. He looked up at John, puzzled at first, then recognition dawning in his eyes.

"Do you recognize him, Steve?"

"Yup."

The man's eyes flicked to Steve. He spat a mouthful of blood and saliva on the floor in his direction.

"*Putain!*"

Steve grinned, the gun still trained on the man's head.

"I bet you didn't expect to see me again, did you, mate?"

"The Algerian. What's his name? Taha?"

Taha looked at John in surprise.

"Yes, I know all about you and your friend. You and your friend... ah... Bogdan were sent to kill me. Well, I've got news for you. That's not going to happen." John knelt and went through his pockets, finding a couple of cable ties in one of the cargo pants pockets and held them up for Steve to see.

"Look what I found."

He rolled Taha over, Taha groaning as the pain from his ribs lanced through his body. Grabbing his left wrist, John secured it to the right and pulled the cable tie tight. Looking down at Taha's legs, he rolled him over again and unlaced his combat boots, removing them before stripping the laces from each and tying his ankles together. He then searched his other pockets, removing the spare magazine and tossing it to Steve, who slipped it into his cargo pocket. John removed a knife strapped to Taha's ankle, slipped it into his own pocket, then

stood up, wiping his hands on his shirt.

"Well, that evens things up."

John stiffened as he heard approaching footsteps. Steve stepped to the side of the door, weapon held at the ready.

Mansur stepped inside, the body of Taha on the floor catching him by surprise. He turned, and his breath caught in his throat as he stared straight down the barrel of the G1.

Steve grinned as he lowered the weapon and slipped the safety on.

"Where have you been, mate? You missed the party."

59

Adriana watched him pace up and down, while her fingers probed under the pillow for the pocketknife she had dropped when he slapped her across the face. Fortunately, the bastard hadn't spotted it in the tent's dim light.

Her fingers felt something hard, and she waited until the man faced away from her, then shifted her position quickly until her fingers got a grasp. Clutching it in her hands, she shifted back just as he turned. She didn't know how much time she had, and she was confident John would come and save her, but she wasn't one to sit around and do nothing. If she could even the odds in her favor—however little—it was worth doing.

She slid the knife down in her left hand and probed the edge with the fingers of her right, feeling for the blade. She was grateful he had fastened her wrists together with the palms facing each other, making things a lot easier. Managing a grip on the top edge of the blade, she squeezed her thumb and forefinger together as hard as she could and gently eased the blade open, all the time her eyes on the man pacing in front of her. He was muttering under his breath, not in French, but what sounded like a Slavic language. His companion had been gone for some time, and he appeared increasingly nervous as he repeatedly checked his watch. Adriana watched him walk to the door, open it a crack, and peer out. She used that moment to switch the knife around, so the blade was facing upwards, then eased it up toward the plastic cable tie. Wincing as the blade scratched her wrist, she adjusted her position until it reached the edge of the plastic. The man closed the door and turned to look at her, the stress clear on his face, even in the poor light. She stopped moving. Turning away, he resumed his pacing.

Adriana started sawing, hoping John had kept the blade sharp.

60

"Is everyone safe?"

"Yes," replied Mansur, still staring at Taha's body on the floor.

"Good. Your daughters?"

Mansur looked up at John. "They're safe, thank you. Everyone's barricaded inside the kitchen building. They locked the doors from the inside, and the shutters have also been closed from the inside. No-one can get in."

"Excellent," John nodded. The odds were now turning in their favor. He crouched beside Taha and slapped his face. "Hey." Taha's eyes opened, and he glared at John, his blood encrusted nostrils flaring. "Do you speak English?"

"A little."

"Good. Now, this can go one of two ways. You can help me, and I'll be lenient, or you can be difficult, and I won't help you. Do you understand?"

"Yes."

"Good. You have to remember, you've taken hostage someone dear to me. You've frightened her, caused her distress. I'm not inclined to help you unless you are very helpful to me. Do you understand?"

"Yes."

"Now, see this man here?" John turned and pointed at Mansur.

Taha's eyes flicked toward Mansur and back at John. He nodded.

"You've taken his wife too. She's Bedouin. Do you know what the Bedouin do to men who dishonor their women?" John had no idea either, but it sounded good.

Taha nodded again.

"So, unless you help me and tell me everything I need to know, I'll leave you alone with him. It won't be pleasant. Think carefully. Look at that knife on his belt and imagine what he will do to you."

Taha's eyes flicked to Mansur again, whose hand had moved to the *Khanjar* on his belt. Taha's shoulders sagged, and he closed his eyes, sighing.

"Okay."

"Good. Here, let me make you more comfortable." John eased Taha up into a seated position and leaned him against the wall.

Taha winced as he moved, settled back against the wall, and stared at his feet. His chest rose up and down as he breathed through his mouth, his shattered nose unable to allow the passage of air.

"Start from the beginning."

Taha licked his lips and coughed, then groaned in pain.

"Hurry up."

"We came from Dubai," Taha started in a mumble. "An Indian man there paid us money to kill you."

"That I've worked out. The man's name?"

"Sss... Surya Patil."

"Go on."

"We drove here." His eyes moved in Steve's direction. "Met him in Bidiyah. He told us where to find you."

"And how did you plan to kill me?"

Taha looked down at the floor.

"We were going to pick you up from your tent early this morning and take you into the desert." He looked up. "We planned to shoot you. The client wanted us to video it and send him the video as proof."

"How much did he pay you?"

"Three hundred thousand U.S. dollars. Half now, half after the video."

Steve let out a low whistle. "I'd do it for that."

John threw a look in his direction, then turned back to Taha.

"Tell me about the other man. The man in the tent."

Taha hesitated, looking at each of the men, reluctant to talk. Mansur's hand moved back to his *Khanjar*, sliding the knife an inch out of the scabbard, exposing part of the highly polished blade.

Taha gulped. "He's a tough man. He won't stop. He was my senior. You know the *Légion Étrangère?*"

John frowned. "The Foreign Legion?"

"Yes," Taha nodded. "We served together. Five years. But he had been in much longer." He swallowed again. "Please, I am helping you. I have family in Algeria. I send them money. Bogdan, he has nothing. He is a dangerous man."

John nodded slowly, almost imperceptibly, studying his face, saying nothing.

"He's armed? Same as you?" he asked after a moment.

"The same weapon. PAMAS G1. Nothing else." He sighed. "We thought this would be easy."

John stood and looked down at him, his hands on his hips, then turned and looked at Mansur and Steve in turn.

"I'm not waiting for the police to get here. The woman I love is inside." He looked at Mansur. "The woman you love is inside."

Mansur nodded, his jaw set, a muscle pulsing in his cheek.

"I'm not leaving them in there a moment longer than necessary."

"What about him?" Steve nodded in Taha's direction.

"He can't go anywhere."

Mansur walked over to Taha and looked down. Taha's face whitened as Mansur slowly unsheathed his *Khanjar*.

"*Non, non,* please," he pleaded.

Mansur squatted down and slipped the tip of the blade under the bottom of Taha's right trouser leg and cut a long slit.

Taha tried to move out of the way, shaking his head, his eyes blinking rapidly. Mansur raised the blade and pointed it at Taha's throat.

"Don't move."

Taha stopped moving, his eyes wide, his breath rapid and uneven.

Mansur cut another slit, then tore off a strip of cloth. He did the same with the other leg while Steve and John watched, unsure what Mansur was doing. Mansur rolled one strip of cloth into a ball, then moved forward, sticking the tip of the *Khanjar* under Taha's chin.

"Open your mouth," he growled.

Taha opened his mouth, and Mansur stuffed the ball of cloth inside, then picked up the other cloth, laying the *Khanjar* on the floor beside him. He quickly and firmly tied the strip around Taha's mouth and head, effectively gagging him. When he finished, he picked up the *Khanjar* and held it against Taha's throat, leaning forward.

"He won't be able to breathe," Steve protested and stepped forward, but John stopped him with a hand on his arm.

"That's his problem," John replied as Mansur leaned forward and muttered something in Arabic in Taha's ear. Taha swallowed and clamped his eyes shut.

Mansur stood, sheathed the blade, and turned to John and Steve.

"*Yalla!*"

61

Adriana felt a snap as the cable ties finally gave way, letting out a slow exhale of relief as she shifted her hands apart slightly, just to make sure. But she wasn't free yet, not by a long shot. Her legs were still fastened, and she wasn't sure how to cut those ties without her captor seeing her. He was getting increasingly anxious, the longer he waited for his companion to return. Adriana glanced over at the travel clock. He had been gone for thirty minutes, longer than needed for him to steal a car. Perhaps he'd been seen? But she'd heard no sound from outside—in fact, the camp was silent.

She edged to the side a little, trying to catch Warda's eye. Her head was just visible past the end of the bed, but she had eyes only for the man who paced back-and-forth while she stared at him intensely as if willing him to drop dead.

The man glanced at his watch again, his forehead creased with concern.

Adriana thought about what she should do next. The more anxious he got, the more dangerous he would become, but... he might also make mistakes. She needed to be ready for whenever he did. She had the knife in her hand, but with bound feet, there wasn't much she could do against a man with a gun. All she could do was wait and hope an opportunity would present itself.

He moved to the door again, cracking it open, peering out toward the reception block, then closed it, cursing under his breath.

To the sides of the tent were two windows covered by wooden shutters which had been kept closed until now. He moved over to the first and putting the weapon back in his waistband, unfastened the bolt holding the shutters closed and slid it open. Swinging the shutters back slowly, he peered out. Seeing nothing, he opened them fully and hooked them to the tent frame at the side. He crossed to the other side, stepping over Warda and did the same.

The open windows allowed cross ventilation, and the breeze, although hot, was welcome, clearing the interior of the stuffy air.

The man moved to the middle of the tent, nudging Warda in the side with his foot until she shifted over, then he stood staring out the mesh netting that covered the window frame. He stood back far enough so no-one could see him, but he still had a clear view outside.

Adriana turned her head too and looked out. From her angle, she could just see past the end of the next tent but could only see open sand. The camp was quiet, not a sound of voices, vehicles, or even activity from the kitchen block. She turned to look back at the man, concern and frustration etched on his face. His right eyelid twitched as he ground his teeth together. Reaching behind him, he pulled out the gun from his waistband, popped the magazine, looked inside, then slid it back home, cocking the weapon as he did so. He bent slightly and patted his left cargo pocket, then reached inside and pulled out a spare magazine, checked it, then slid it back into his pocket. His head moved left to right, constantly checking the view from the windows, the weapon hanging at his side as he rocked back-and-forth on the balls of his feet.

Adriana closed her eyes and said a small prayer. If she got out of this alive, she would be much more diligent about attending church. Exhaling slowly, she opened her eyes and felt the reassuring shape of the pocketknife in her hand, the blade still extended.

Looking down at Warda, she finally caught her eye. She gave her a wink, and although duct tape covered her mouth, gave her a reassuring smile, trusting her eyes would send enough of a message.

62

The three men conferred on the far side of the reception block, out of Taha's earshot.

"We know he's armed and has plenty of ammunition."

Steve and Mansur nodded.

"He has two hostages, and we have to assume he can see anyone approaching the tent. There are windows on both sides and the door to the front. There's also a sliding window at the front. So, he has visibility on three sides."

"So, we approach from the back?" suggested Mansur

"We could," John nodded, mentally calculating the risks, "but there's still a chance he'll see us. He can see the reception building from the tent. As soon as we step out, we'll be spotted." John shook his head. "I don't like it. It's too risky."

"Why don't we use him?" Steve asked nodding in Taha's direction. "We could send him down there to distract his partner while we go around the back."

All three men turned to look at Taha.

"Look at the state of his face, and besides, why would he do it?" John asked.

"You heard him, he wants us to go easy on him, that's why he answered your questions."

"Huh," Mansur snorted. "I don't trust him. He's a Berber."

Steve raised an eyebrow and glanced at Mansur. "I thought he was Arab like you?"

"I'm Bedouin. He's not like me," Mansur shook his head.

Steve shrugged.

"I don't trust him either," John interrupted. "The men have served together. That's a bond you can't break."

"But he was answering your questions," Steve countered.

"Steve, he told us nothing we didn't already know. He saw you here. He would have guessed you'd told us everything. No, he was just buying time. Saving himself a little pain."

"Yeah, you could be right, mate," Steve nodded slowly. "But I still say we can use him. We keep the gun trained on him. If he says or does anything wrong, we put a bullet in him."

John turned and studied Steve's face.

"What happened to the ex-cop? How do you plan to explain to the Royal Oman Police you shot an unarmed man?"

"Yeah, mate, I guess I'm just getting excited," Steve grinned.

"Besides, have you fired a handgun before?"

"Many times." Steve hesitated. "On the range."

"Ever shot a man?"

"No."

"Trust me, you don't want to."

Mansur glanced at John with interest but said nothing.

"Besides," John continued, "what's the effective range of

a weapon like that." He nodded toward the G1 in Steve's hand.

"Dunno, mate. Maybe fifty meters?"

"The tent is over a hundred meters away. Even if you could make the shot, what would happen next?"

"He would execute my wife," Mansur spoke up, then looked at John, "and yours."

"Yeah," Steve sighed.

John rested his hands on his hips and stared at the wall in front of him. The fan overhead creaked as it turned lazily, doing nothing to cool the room. A warm breeze blew off the dunes and through the open reception, carrying sand across the floor.

John turned to the two men.

"I'll go. I'll keep him talking. You two approach from the back."

"Then what?" Steve questioned. "He can still shoot you. Then his job is done."

"True," John shrugged then a light bulb went off in his head. He looked over at Taha. "I'll take some insurance."

63

John closed his eyes and calmed his breathing. What he was doing was suicidal, but he couldn't sit around and do nothing while Adriana was held captive. Opening his eyes, he raised the semi-automatic and pressed the muzzle into Taha's back.

"Start walking."

Taha stepped through the doorway onto the sandy path, hopping from side-to-side as his bare feet got used to the hot sand, then started walking toward the far tent. John had unfastened his ankles but kept his hands bound and his mouth gagged. He walked behind, making sure Taha's body remained as a shield between him and the tent.

As he approached the tent, his heart hammered away, and his hands became clammy, moist with sweat. He gripped the G1 tighter and once again, prodded Taha in the back.

"Remember what I told you. If you behave, I'll let you go," he hissed.

Taha grunted and walked a little faster. Thirty meters from the tent, John instructed Taha to stop. Stepping closer to him, he grabbed a handful of the back of his shirt and brought the barrel of the gun up to the side of Taha's head.

"Bogdan Kolisnick," he called out.

There was no reply, but through the mesh covering the windows, he saw a change in the way the light filtered through as if someone was moving around inside.

"Bogdan Kolisnick. I know you're inside. I know who you are. I know what you want."

John heard a curse from inside, then he saw the door open slightly.

"Taha, *ca va?*"

"Taha can't talk right now, Bogdan."

John heard another curse from inside.

"Let the ladies go, Bogdan. They have nothing to do with this. It's me you want."

"*Putain!*"

John saw a metal cylinder poke through the crack in the door, then a gunshot. He flinched but kept Taha in front of him as a fountain of sand erupted beside his feet. Taha's leg shook, and John had to use all his strength to keep him standing.

"I'll shoot him, Bogdan. I'm not afraid. And after I shoot him, I'll come for you. So, I'm telling you again. Let the women go."

The door closed, and there was the sound of movement from inside. A movement near the rear of the tent caught John's eye. Glancing over, he saw Steve and Mansur moving into position, staying close to the tent wall, behind the windows. The door swung open, and Adriana and Warda filled the doorway, Warda's hands bound in front while Adriana's appeared to be fastened behind her. John's chest contracted, and his grip on Taha tightened. Adriana's eyes met his, and she thrust her chin forward and gave a slight nod. John's vision narrowed down, all his senses focused on the scene. Bogdan's head moved forward into the light, the barrel of his gun appearing between the two women, pointed in John's direction.

"John Hayes. You let my friend go, and I will release the women."

John ground his teeth together, deciding what to do. It broke his heart to see Adriana treated like this—she didn't deserve it. It was all his fault, but he knew the minute he let Taha go, he would get a bullet in the head.

"No," he called out. "I don't trust you."

"Then I'll kill one of them."

"The minute you do that Bogdan, Taha dies. And the next bullet will be for you."

Bogdan cursed again.

John saw Steve creep forward. He gave a slight shake of his head, and Steve stopped moving. It was still too risky, too many people could die.

"Get me a vehicle, and I'll let them go."

"Okay," John agreed, buying for time. "But how do I know you'll keep your word?"

"Bring the vehicle here. I will let one of them go. Then I'll drive one hundred meters from here and stop. You let Taha go, and I will let the other one go, at the same time."

John chewed his lip, thinking it over. He still didn't trust him, but it might be a way to end the stalemate.

He glanced over at Steve and nodded. Steve straightened up and edged toward the back of the tent, then turned and ran.

64

Steve ran through the reception building and out into the parking. Reaching into his pocket, he pulled out the key for the Pajero, and as he did so, his eye fell on the battered, sand-colored Toyota pickup parked to one side. He walked over and glanced inside. The load tray was empty, as was the cabin. He looked back at the Pajero, filled with water and supplies and got an idea. He tried the door handle of the pickup. It opened. Leaning inside, he checked for the keys, but they weren't there. He jogged back to the reception and crossed to the reception desk, searching the desktop for any sign of the keys. He pulled out the drawer and scanned the detritus strewn inside. Finding a set of keys with a Toyota logo stamped on the side, he grabbed it and ran back outside, climbing into the pickup and started it up. There was a roar and a puff of black smoke from the back before it settled into a rough idle. Steve glanced down at the fuel gauge. Only a quarter of a tank—even better, no water and no fuel. No point in making things easy for the intruders. He selected a gear, did a three-point turn, then headed in the direction of the tents.

65

John stood, watching Bogdan, then moved his eyes across to Adriana. She was staring straight at him as if trying to get his attention. Her chin was held high, no sign of fear in her eyes. He looked at Warda. It was the first time he had seen her without her hair and face hidden by the *hijab* and *niqab*. She was an attractive woman with a proud face, but there was no sign of the mischievous nature they had glimpsed last night. She didn't look scared, more angry, and John pitied the man who got on the wrong side of her.

John heard the engine and glanced toward the pickup grinding its way through the sand toward them. John nodded in appreciation, realizing why Steve had chosen it. Steve drove the vehicle around behind John and pulled up next to the tent. Leaving the engine running, he climbed out, leaving the driver's door open, then backed away behind the tent, keeping out of Bogdan's line of fire.

"We brought the car, Bogdan, now let one of the ladies go."

Bogdan pushed the two women out the door, and they

stepped onto the sand. He kept behind them and pointed the gun barrel first at Adriana's head, then Warda's.

"Which one do you want Mr. Hayes? This one?" He pointed the barrel at Adriana again. "Or the Arab?" He switched the barrel to Warda's head.

"Don't play games, Bogdan." John felt sick and looked at Adriana again, "Let one of them go."

John almost thought he imagined it, but Adriana gave him a slight nod, then things happened quickly.

Before he could react, Adriana dropped to her knees, her arms came up from behind her back, and she thrust her right hand toward Bogdan's thigh.

66

Bogdan screamed and swung his left hand back, striking Adriana on the side of the head, knocking her to the ground. John stepped forward as Adriana rolled away, but before he could do anything, Bogdan had brought his hand forward again, grabbing Warda's hair and pulled her toward him, shoving the barrel of his weapon into the side of her head.

"Get back!" he screamed as blood spurted from the wound in his leg. John narrowed his eyes. It looked suspiciously like his pocketknife sticking out of the man's thigh. Adriana shook her head, half sat up, then wriggled away from Bogdan. She felt a pair of hands grab her arms from behind, pulling her behind the tent. She struggled to get free, then looked up into Mansur's grim face. He held a finger to his lips, then left her there and stepped back toward the corner of the tent.

Bogdan moved backward, pulling Warda with him.

"Stay back! I'll kill her," he screamed, the whites of his eyes flashing wildly as he looked side-to-side. He moved past the edge of the tent and saw Mansur. Wrenching Warda around, so Mansur could see the gun pressed to her temple, he yelled. "I'll kill her! Get back!"

Mansur retreated, his hands raised in the air, his eyes meeting Warda's, rage growing like a furnace in his belly.

Bogdan continued walking sideways toward the pickup, his eyes darting from John to Mansur and back. He backed up against the vehicle, then moved sideways until he could slide into the driver's seat. Letting go of Warda's hair, in one movement he slipped his arm around her waist, and pulled her in after him. He shoved the gear lever into Drive and stomped on the gas, the driver's door swinging closed and banging onto Warda's legs still hanging out the door. John, Mansur, Steve, and Adriana watched it move away across the sand, expecting it to stop any moment, to make the exchange with Taha. It passed fifty meters and kept going; one hundred meters, still no sign of stopping. Mansur cried out in anguish, holding his hands to his head. John loosened his grip on Taha, and Taha dropped to his knees, then slumped back on his haunches, resigned to the betrayal.

"Fuck!" yelled John. He swung the barrel of the PAMAS into the side of Taha's head, knocking him flat on the ground, then sprinted toward Adriana.

67

Mansur ran toward him and pulled the weapon from John's hand as he dropped to his knees in the sand, throwing his arms around Adriana. He held her close, rocking back and forward, his face buried in her hair.

"I'm so sorry, I'm so sorry. You're safe now. You're safe," he murmured into her hair. He pulled his head away and kissed her forehead, then held her face in both hands, staring into her eyes. "Are you okay? Did he hurt you?"

Adriana shook her head and smiled, her eyes moist. John pulled her close again, pressing her face into his shoulder. He looked over her head to see Mansur sprinting across the desert after the pickup. John pulled away for a second time and looked into her eyes.

"I have to go. I have to help Mansur. We must save Warda."

Adriana frowned, then gave a small nod, a tear trickling from the corner of her left eye.

John looked up at Steve. "Steve, please take care of her. I'll go after Mansur."

Steve gave him a thumbs up.

"The pickup only has a quarter tank of fuel. I don't know how far he'll get."

John nodded and looked back at Adriana.

"Stay here with Steve. He's a good man, he'll keep you safe."

"Be careful, John." Adriana wiped her cheek with the back of her hand. "You'd better come back."

John stood up and helped Adriana to her feet.

"I promise."

Turning back to Steve, he continued, "The police will be here in less than three hours."

"Yeah," Steve nodded.

John paused and studied Steve's face.

"Maybe they don't need to know everything?"

"I'll handle it," Steve grinned, reached forward, and patted John's shoulder. "I'm an ex-cop. I know what to say."

"Thank you. I owe you a beer."

"Ha, you owe me a bloody brewery, mate." Steve waved toward Taha still lying in the sand, blood seeping from the split skin on the side of his head. "What do we do with him?"

"I'll leave that up to you." He sighed, looked at Adriana, then back at Steve. "I need the Pajero keys." He stepped closer to Steve, and as Steve removed the keys from his pocket, John leaned in and in a low voice spoke, "Whatever you decide, do it before you release the staff from the kitchen block."

He straightened, fixing Steve in his gaze, not sure if he understood. Steve gave a nod, and John turned back, kissed Adriana on her forehead, then turned and sprinted toward the parking and the Pajero.

68

John unlocked the Pajero as he approached and jumped inside. Starting the engine, he threw the vehicle in reverse, then swung it around before heading off across the parking area toward the track. He drove as fast as he could, circumnavigating the camp until he reached the rear, then picked up the trail leading deeper into the desert. Ahead, he could see Mansur still running, and far in the distance, the shape of the pickup, getting smaller and smaller as it headed up the wide valley between the dunes. Mansur glanced over his shoulder as John approached, then when John pulled up, ran around to the driver's side, wrenching open the door.

"Move over, John!" John slid across to the passenger seat as Mansur handed him the PAMAS and gunned the engine. He set off at a speed John could never have maintained, years of experience giving him an instinctive knowledge of where to place the vehicle and which areas to avoid. His chest rose and fell as he regained his breath from the sprint across the desert, his forehead set in a frown of concentration, eyes scanning the surface ahead constantly.

John looked ahead at the pickup. They were gaining on it, and as they neared, they could see it swerving from side-to-side, the driver's door still not closed. Suddenly, it swung violently from right to left and back again. Mansur gasped as a body rolled out the door onto the sand, tumbling over and over.

"Warda!" he cried out and accelerated even harder. The pickup slowed to a stop, and the driver's door opened fully. They saw Bogdan lean out and raise his gun barrel, pointing it in the body's direction.

John thrust his arm out the window, pointed the PAMAS at him, and fired. The shot went wide as the Pajero bucked and swayed in the sand, Mansur not slowing, desperate to get to Warda before Bogdan shot her. John fired again, this time lucky, the rear window of the pickup's cab shattering. Bogdan ducked back inside, and the pickup accelerated away.

Mansur slammed on the brakes and pulled up beside the body as the pickup disappeared in the distance. He leaped out before the vehicle had come to a complete stop, rushing to the crumpled form lying in the sand. John jumped out, let off another couple of shots in the pickup's direction before running around the vehicle to where Mansur was kneeling, cradling Warda in his arms. She had blood on her face and arms and dark stains across her *abaya*.

"Is she okay?"

John crouched down and with relief, saw Warda's eyes open, looking up at Mansur. Tears filled her eyes as Mansur's also welled with emotion.

Mansur looked up. "She's okay. The blood is his."

John exhaled loudly, his shoulders relaxing. Closing his eyes, he took a deep breath before releasing it again and mentally said thank you. Everyone was safe now

Warda said something in Arabic, and Mansur looked down and replied.

"What's she saying?"

"She said we have to kill him."

John nodded and looked toward the pickup as Mansur got to his feet and tenderly helped Warda stand, her hands still bound. Mansur unsheathed his *Khanjar* and cut the cable ties. Rubbing her wrists, she stared after the pickup and spat in the sand. Looking at both the men she said, *"Yalla!"* and strode toward the Pajero.

The three of them climbed back in, and Mansur set off in pursuit.

"What's in that direction?" John asked, nodding toward the pickup.

"Nothing for two hundred kilometers," Mansur growled, his arms wrestling with the steering, fighting for traction. "But eventually, he will reach the coast and the highway. We have to stop him before then."

"He only has a quarter tank of diesel left."

"Good." Mansur gave a grim smile. "He won't make it."

Mansur's superior driving skill helped them make up ground, and they were within one hundred meters of the pickup and closing when Mansur spoke up again.

"He will get stuck."

Warda spoke up from the rear seat, and Mansur nodded and grinned without mirth, glancing at John.

"Warda says he's losing a lot of blood." He slowed and let the distance between them increase.

"What are you doing?"

"We wait, he'll get stuck. You'll see."

They followed the pickup for another fifteen minutes, hanging back, Mansur taking a different line now and then to maintain traction, then...

"Ha. See how the color of that sand is a little different? Where he's heading is deep. He's good, but he doesn't know the sand like the Bedouin." He slowed to a stop and selected low ratio and activated the diff-lock. Moving off again at a low speed, John fretted they would lose the pickup again as the distance increased.

"Don't worry, John. Be patient."

Five minutes later, the pickup visibly slowed, then stopped. Mansur also stopped and chuckled.

"I've got you now, *sharmouta*."

Sand sprayed up from behind the pickup as the wheels spun, fighting for traction. Slowly, the vehicle moved forward until it bogged down again, the tires now axle deep in the sand. Black clouds of diesel smoke rose in the air as Bogdan desperately gunned the engine, to no avail.

"He won't get out of there," Mansur shook his head.

The driver's door opened, and Bogdan stepped out, the left leg of his cargo pants stained black. He held onto the side of the pickup as he raised his right hand and let off a shot in their direction.

"Pull back, pull back!" John urged. "Stay out of range!"

Mansur selected reverse and swiftly and skillfully reversed down the dune and out of sight around the side before stopping. John jumped out and climbed the dune beside them. Reaching the top, he dropped onto his stomach and looked down at the pickup. Mansur and Warda dropped beside him, the three of them breathing hard from the exertion.

Below them, Bogdan limped around the vehicle, looking

at each of the wheels. He shook his head, raised his hands in the air, and cried out in frustration.

"What do we do?" asked Mansur.

John looked up at the sky, the sun now directly overhead, its heat scorching them like a blowtorch.

"How far will a man get on foot? Without water?"

"Not far."

John nodded thoughtfully. "He can shelter under the vehicle."

Mansur made a face. "It won't help him much. He's wounded."

"Let's wait then." John looked over at Mansur. "I don't feel like being shot today."

Mansur nodded and translated for Warda, who scowled and glared toward Bogdan.

John wiped his face with the *shemagh*, slid out of sight, down the face of the dune, and stood up.

"Keep an eye on him. I'll get some water." He handed the PAMAS to Mansur, slid, then jumped down the dune toward the Pajero. Opening the back, he pulled out a couple of bottles of water, opened one, and took a long pull. A hot breeze funneled down between the dunes, drying his eyeballs and spraying hot grains of sand against his face. He turned his back on it, pulled the ends of his *shemagh* around his neck, and drained the bottle before tossing it in the back. He looked at his watch and did a mental calculation. It had been about an hour since the German couple had left. The police would reach the camp in another two hours. John and Mansur had driven for thirty minutes into the desert. If the police followed them, they would reach them in another two-and-a-half, maybe three hours. John looked up at the two figures lying on top of the dune. He was hoping Steve understood his hint about Taha, but he couldn't afford for the police to find out why Bogdan had been following him. Bogdan was weak and dehydrated, but would he survive until the police arrived? It was a risk—not one John wanted to take. He picked up the water bottles, closed the tailgate, and headed back up the slope. He would have to do something.

69

John dropped to his knees, below the rim of the dune, then crawled forward. Passing a bottle to both Mansur and Warda, they slid down out of sight and sat up, unscrewing the bottle tops, and drinking thirstily. John watched them, then addressed Mansur.

"The police could be here soon."

Mansur nodded, watching John's face but saying nothing as Warda listened.

"It would be better for me if they didn't find that man alive."

Mansur nodded and took another mouthful of water.

"We need to speed things up."

John held his hand out for the handgun. Mansur handed it over with a frown.

"What's your plan?"

John crawled to the lip of the dune and looked down. Bogdan was sitting in the sand, his head slumped on his chest, his back leaning against the pickup, the shade from the vehicle giving him some respite from the sun.

John raised the PAMAS, took aim, and fired, a spurt of sand rising into the air next to Bogdan. He looked up with a start, raised his pistol and fired. John ducked down as a bullet whizzed overhead, then fired another round at Bogdan, sending him crawling through the sand to the other side of the vehicle.

"You missed," accused Mansur. "Twice."

"No, I didn't," John grinned. "I can't shoot him—too many questions afterward—but I can get him out of the shade."

Mansur grinned back and translated for Warda, who smiled for the first time since she was captured.

John looked at his watch.

"You two go down and rest. It's too hot to stay up here. We'll take turns keeping an eye on him. Let's do... thirty minutes each?"

Mansur nodded and explained to Warda, then they turned and made their way down the dune toward the Pajero, Mansur holding Warda close as if afraid to lose her again.

John returned his attention to the pickup. Bogdan couldn't be seen, but there were no tracks leading away from the vehicle, so John assumed he was still hiding around the other side.

John ducked down below the edge and stood up, making his way along the dune to get a better view. A hundred meters further along, he lowered himself to the ground, then crawled up to peer over the top. He could just see Bogdan's legs jutting out from the side of the pickup where he was sitting in the sand, but John still wasn't at a good angle to see his whole body. John looked to his left to see if he could continue around and get a view from the other side, but there was a gap between the dunes that would leave him exposed and wasn't worth the risk. He would continue to wait. Pulling the ends of his *shemagh* to protect the sides of his face from the scorching sun, he pulled the sleeves of his shirt down to cover any exposed skin and settled down for a long wait.

70

After half an hour, with no sign of movement from the pickup, he heard Mansur approaching and looked up. Mansur slid in beside him and handed him another bottle of water.

"Anything happening?"

"Nothing," replied John as he opened the bottle and took a sip. He looked over his shoulder toward the Pajero. "Will she be okay?"

Mansur didn't respond immediately, his eyes fixed on the pickup below.

"I think so," he said, after a moment. "She's a strong woman, John." He looked at John. "*Alhamdulilah,* he didn't do anything to her."

"That's good." John reached over and placed his hand on Mansur's arm. "Look, I'm sorry. It's my fault this happened." John swallowed. "I will never forget the help you've given me. You saved my life. You saved Adriana's life. If I can ever repay you, I will."

"It's all God's will, my friend," Mansur smiled.

"If you say so. I'm not a believer, but I know I couldn't have done this without you and Steve."

Mansur smiled and jerked his head toward the pickup.

"It's not over yet."

John nodded and looked at his watch, chewing his lip.

"I'm going down there."

"I'm coming with you."

"No. You've risked enough already but take this." John passed over the weapon. "If anything happens... shoot him."

John got to his feet and with one last glance at Mansur, made his way slowly and silently down the dune.

He reached the bottom and waited, straining his ears for any sign Bogdan had heard him. He'd been quiet, the sand absorbing any sound he'd made and was confident he hadn't been heard. He looked up at Mansur, who gave him a thumbs up. Taking a deep breath, he stepped forward and approached the vehicle. He couldn't see Bogdan, the vehicle buried to its chassis in the sand. He kept low in case Bogdan got up and saw him through the glass, although John thought it unlikely. He hadn't moved in the last thirty minutes.

John reached the vehicle and stopped, listening, but there was no sound. Keeping low, he crept to the rear of the vehicle, then peered around the back. He saw Bogdan's boots, then his legs. His right hand rested in the sand, his G1 lying on the sand beside it. John leaned forward even more and saw Bogdan's torso and his head, chin resting on his chest, his eyes closed, his chest rising slowly up and down.

He was alive but looked weak. John leaned back and thought quickly, looking at his watch again. He had to end this before the cops arrived. Stepping forward, he rounded the end of the car and took another step closer to Bogdan. One more step and Bogdan's eyes opened. John dove forward, his hand reaching for the G1. He grabbed the barrel and rolled out of the way, pulling the weapon toward him, fumbling with it until it pointed in the right direction. But he needn't have bothered. Bogdan blinked at him, no attempt to move. His lips were cracked, his face reddened by the sun, his chest rising and falling as he took his last breaths. John stood up and keeping the gun pointing at him, moved closer until he was standing above him. Bloodstained sand encrusted the stab wound on his thigh.

John looked down with disgust. He stepped forward and placed the sole of his boot on Bogdan's thigh and pressed down on the wound.

Bogdan croaked in pain and grasped John's ankle with his left hand. John shook it free with little difficulty, Bogdan no longer having any strength. Bogdan's lips moved soundlessly, and John squatted down, still keeping the weapon ready, in case it was a trick.

Bogdan's lips moved again, and John leaned forward.

"Water... water," came the hoarse croak.

"You come after me, you kidnap the woman I love... and now, you want water?" John sneered. He shook his head and thrust the barrel of the G1 into Bogdan's leg wound and twisted it. "Fuck you!"

This time the scream of pain was audible, and John twisted the barrel again for good measure as Bogdan fell to his side on the sand, whimpering in pain. John wiped the barrel on Bogdan's shirt and stood up. He looked up toward the top of the dune where Mansur was now standing, looking down with concern. He raised a hand in reassurance, then looked at Bogdan again. He was pretty far gone and would be unlikely to last the night. He looked at his watch—time to get moving before the police arrived. He stepped away and slipped the G1 into his waistband. At the front of the pickup, he stopped and looked back—he had to make sure.

He turned back and walked toward Bogdan. Kneeling on the sand, he grabbed Bogdan by the hair and dragged him away from the vehicle, Bogdan protesting weakly. John looked up to ensure he was out of sight of Mansur, then bent down and flipped him over until he was face down in the sand. Sitting astride him, he pressed Bogdan's face into the sand, holding him down as he began to kick and thrash about with his arms. John kept pushing down, the veins in his forearms standing out like cords as the struggle from Bogdan became weaker and weaker until it stopped altogether. John held him for another thirty seconds, then slowly released his grip.

With two fingers of his right hand, he felt for a pulse on the side of Bogdan's neck, and satisfied there was no pulse, he searched through Bogdan's pockets. He found an iPhone and unlocked it using Bogdan's thumb before changing the settings and password to one he would remember. Pocketing it, he removed the G1 from his waistband, wiped it clean with Bogdan's shirt, then dropped it in the sand beside the body. He got to his feet and brushed off his pants, walking around the vehicle, and climbed back up the dune.

Mansur watched him approach, saying nothing. John stopped in front of him, turning to look back down the dune.

"It's over."

Mansur studied his face for a moment, then nodded, and together, they made the descent down the other side toward the Pajero.

71

They rode back in silence at a much slower speed, grateful for the air-conditioning. Mansur concentrated on the route ahead, and John glanced over his shoulder at Warda, who sat, gazing out the side window. As they reached the camp, a sand-colored SUV approached them on the track. Mansur slowed and pulled up alongside, winding down the window to have a conversation in Arabic with the two policemen who sat inside. Their eyes flicked to John and Warda a couple of times while they asked questions, then they carried on, and Mansur wound up the window, looking at John.

"I told them where to find his body."

John narrowed his eyes.

"I told them he was dead when we got there. Dehydration and loss of blood."

"Good. *Shukraan.*"

"*Afwan,* you are welcome, my friend."

Mansur drove on, and they entered the parking for the camp. Beside John's Land Cruiser were another two police SUV's and a second white Land Cruiser. John recognized the German couple's driver standing beside it. Mansur parked, and they climbed out. A cry from the reception building and the two small figures of Mansur's daughters came running toward them. Warda and Mansur ran over, Mansur picking them both up at the same time in a giant bear hug, spinning around as Warda looked on, tears of relief streaming down her face. John turned to the driver, Tariq.

"Thank you. Did Gunther and Johanna get away safely?"

"They are here," Tariq replied and waved toward the reception building.

"What?" John stepped forward and entered the building to find Gunther and Johanna sitting on either side of Adriana while a group of policemen stood, talking to Steve. Adriana stood and rushed toward him, and John pulled her close in a tight embrace, nodding his thanks to Gunther over her shoulder

"Oh, thank God, John."

"It's okay. He'll never bother you again."

Adriana pulled away, her eyes wide.

"You...?"

"He was dead when we found him. Loss of blood and dehydration. His vehicle was stuck in the sand." John glanced at the policemen who were watching with interest. "I'll tell you everything later."

John loosened his grip on Adriana as a smartly dressed police officer stepped toward him, his hand outstretched in greeting.

"I am Captain Al-Harthi of the Royal Oman Police."

John shook his hand, the Captain's grip firm, his expression serious but not unkind.

"John Hayes."

"Yes, Mr. Jones here,"—he nodded in Steve's direction

—"has explained what happened. I am very sorry it has disturbed your holiday in this way." His eyes darted over John's shoulder as Mansur and Warda stepped inside with the girls. Adriana rushed over and embraced Warda while Mansur stepped forward and shook the Captain's hand.

"As salaam aleikum."

"Wa aleikum a salaam."

Mansur and Captain Al-Harthi started a conversation in Arabic, and John used the opportunity to step closer to Steve, leaning in, whispering in Steve's ear.

"Taha?"

"Never heard of him, mate."

"I believe we have you to thank, Mr. Hayes," Captain Al-Harthi switched to English. He nodded toward Mansur and continued, "Mr. Wahibi here says you helped save his wife's life. We are very grateful to you. I am sorry, as a guest of our country, you have had to endure this, and please be assured, we will do everything we can to make sure this does not happen again."

"It's okay. It all ended well. He won't be bothering anyone again. Your men will be recovering his body as we speak."

Captain Al-Harthi nodded thoughtfully. "The desert is a cruel place, Mr. Hayes. There are few who can survive here." He frowned and looked straight at John. "One question, though. Was there one man or two? Because the German couple said there were two."

John avoided looking in Steve's direction.

"We were wrong. There was only one, thankfully. If not, I don't think Adriana would have been able to overpower him."

The Captain nodded slowly, then broke eye contact and smiled at Adriana.

"Your wife is a brave woman."

John made to correct him about their marital status, then closed his mouth. It wouldn't make a difference. He turned and smiled at Adriana.

"Yes, my wife is very brave. I'm a lucky man."

72

It was three hours before the police finished taking statements from the staff, and the body of Bogdan had been returned to the camp. John, Steve, and Mansur had forgotten to mention Bogdan and Taha's Land Cruiser abandoned in the desert, so consequently, the police had failed to look for it. Mansur told John he would strip it down and use it for parts, and no-one would ever need to know. Toyota parts were easy to dispose of, most Bedouin owning a Land Cruiser of some sort.

The staff rearranged the bookings for that day and kindly allowed John, Adriana, and Steve to stay another night. Gunther and Johanna had stayed as well, horrified at what had happened, eager to provide comfort and support.

Alone, at last, John took Adriana by the hand and led her back to their tent. Stepping inside, they were happy to see the staff had cleaned it up and removed all trace of the morning's invasion. A bowl of dates and a fresh pot of Omani coffee in a silver urn sat on a silver platter, and the sweet fragrance of *Frankincense* and *Oudh* filled the air, tiny tendrils of smoke spiraling up from a terracotta burner in the corner.

John kicked off his boots and took Adriana in his arms.

"Are you okay?" he murmured into her hair.

Adriana pulled away and studied his face, looking from eye to eye.

"No, John, I'm not okay. Who were those men?"

John shrugged and looked away. Letting her go, he walked over to the coffee table and looked down at the bowl of dates.

"John, look at me. I need you to be honest with me."

John turned to face her, his heart sinking, a deep sadness coming over him. He loved this woman, but would she still love him if he told her the truth about his past? He'd been putting it off, dreading the moment when he would have to come clean.

"John, I know something bad happened in your past, that you lost your wife. I know it must have been terrible, but please talk to me." She raised her hands in frustration, then dropped them down again. "I love you, John. I want to spend the rest of my life with you, but I need you to trust me."

John sighed, a heavy knot growing in his stomach. He shook his head and looked down, studying the rug at his feet, anything to avoid saying something.

Adriana stepped forward and held his arms, lowering her voice.

"John, you have to tell me. I want to know everything about you. I think we owe that to each other. Tell me, why were these men after you? What have you done?"

John gritted his teeth, closed his eyes, then let out a long breath. Opening them again, he looked Adriana in the eye.

"I'll tell you, but you'd better sit down."

Adriana nodded and sat down on the edge of the bed, her hands resting on the bed beside her legs, her bare feet crossed at the ankle.

"You know I lost my wife."

Adriana nodded, then tilted her head to one side, a slight frown on her forehead.

"I never told you what happened." Taking a deep breath, he walked across the tent, turned and paced back again, his eyes filling with tears as the deeply buried memories came to the surface. He stopped and turned to face Adriana.

"Charlotte was kidnapped, gang-raped, then murdered, her body dumped in a ditch."

"Oh my God, John." Adriana's mouth dropped open in shock, and her hand raised to cover her mouth. "I'm so sorry, John. I'm so sorry." She jumped to her feet and threw her arms around him, pulling him into a tight embrace, her face buried against his shoulder. "I'm so, so sorry."

Tears ran down John's face, and he started to sob silently, his body shaking and shuddering.

"It's okay, it's okay," murmured Adriana as she ran her hands up and down his back. "Now I know why you keep having nightmares."

"No," John pulled away and held her at arm's length.

"What do you mean?"

John let go of her and wiped his nose with the back of his hand.

"That's not why I have nightmares."

Adriana frowned. "Then, why?"

"Because I found out who did it, hunted them down, and killed every last one of them," he blurted out.

Adriana's eyes widened, her mouth open.

"That's why I have nightmares. I don't see my wife's face anymore, I see theirs. Each one of them, haunting my sleep.

I thought they'd gone once I met you, but..." John shook his head and sighed. "They came back."

Adriana sat back on the bed, stunned, not sure what to say.

John continued, his fear of losing Adriana pushed aside by the sheer relief of finally telling someone what happened.

"The Police knew who it was, but they couldn't do anything. There was political pressure to keep it quiet. One of them was a politician's son. They were rich. They had power." John shrugged. "I didn't plan it... at first. The first was an accident, but then I thought, why not? Why should they get away with it while my Charlotte rots in a ditch? So, I killed them," he shrugged. John paced up and down, not even looking at Adriana for fear of what he would see.

"The father, the politician, Surya Patil, somehow found out I was in Dubai. He paid Steve to follow us. He sent those two men to kill me." He turned back to face Adriana. "They were instructed to take me out into the desert, kill me, video the killing, and send it to him. They failed..." His voice trailed off, running out of steam as he noticed the expression on Adriana's face.

"Baby, I'm sorry. I never knew this would happen. I never want any harm to come to you."

Adriana stood up. "I need some time to think," she said, walking out of the tent.

John's heart cracked. He knew he had lost her. He watched her walk away across the sand and climb the dune, leaving a trail of footprints across the pristine, sandy slope. She reached the top and stopped, silhouetted against the pink-hued evening sky, then disappeared from sight over the other side

John clenched his fists and ground his teeth. Once again,

he had lost the woman he loved because of the motherfucking Patil family! First, the son, now the father. Could he ever leave his past behind?

He flexed his fingers and rubbed his face, exhausted and empty. If it was the last thing he did on this planet, he would make sure every last one of the Patils was wiped out.

73

It was half an hour before she returned. He watched her approach from the chair he had set up in the sand outside the tent. It was getting dark, but her walk was unmistakable—the gentle sway of her hips, her long legs, her hair blowing gently in the evening breeze which wafted in over the dunes. She stopped in front of him, and he waited, looking up at her, his breath caught in his throat, scared of what she might say. She reached out for his hand, and he stood, holding her hand in his. Taking his other hand, she stared straight into his eyes. John still didn't breathe, terrified... then she smiled. He breathed out, the tension flowing out of his neck and shoulders.

"I love you, John Hayes. I love everything about you. Whatever you have done, whatever you will do. But you have to promise me one thing."

A tear rolled down John's cheek.

"Anything."

"No more secrets."

"No more secrets."

She pulled him closer, lifting her lips to his. John

melted, his arms wrapping around her, pulling her body into his until they became one.

Adriana pulled her head away, a glint in her eye,

"Oh, one more thing..."

John raised an eyebrow.

"What?"

"You need to finish this."

74

"Welcome back, my friend. You are a day late."

John smiled and put his hand out the window to shake hands with Ahmed.

"Ahmed, my friend, it's good to see you again. Yes, we loved the desert and stayed back."

Ahmed glanced behind them to where Steve had just pulled up at his tire shop in the Pajero.

"Ah, I am happy your friend found you."

John glanced in the rearview mirror and nodded.

"Yes, so am I."

He stepped out of the car as Ahmed's mechanics busied themselves returning the Land Cruiser's tires to their normal pressure. Walking back to the Pajero, he reached in and shook Steve's hand.

"Thank you, Steve... for everything."

"You're welcome, mate. You still owe me a beer."

"Ha," John laughed. "I don't think you'll get a beer in Bidiyah. Where are you headed to now?"

"Back to Muscat, mate, then on the first flight to Dubai. You?"

"We'll stick around. We'll head up into the mountains, for some cool air. Spend some time together. Repair the damage."

"Yeah, good idea, mate." He handed John a business card, "Next time you're in Dubai, look me up. Hopefully, I'll still be in business. I never sent my last bill to Surya Patil, so I'm gonna have to knuckle down and earn the money back." He grinned, "I have an expensive ex-wife."

John studied the card then looked up. "Steve, we never discussed Taha."

"Who?"

John frowned. "I'm serious. Adriana said you let him go?"

"That's what I told her."

"Is she correct?"

Steve sighed and stared out the windscreen, "It's better she believes that." He turned and looked at John. "Let's just say I don't like loose ends, and I'm sure you don't either."

John studied his face for a while, then smiled. "Thank you, Steve." He looked down at Steve's card again. "Look... why don't you send your last bill to me? I'll take care of it. It's the least I can do, and it's probably cheaper than having a few beers with you. I know what you Aussies are like."

"Thanks, mate, I appreciate it. I mean it." He reached through the window and shook John's hand. "You take care of that lovely lady of yours. She's a keeper."

John smiled and looked toward the Land Cruiser again. "She sure is, Steve, she sure is."

Ahmed approached and banged on the hood of the Pajero. "All done, my friends."

"Thank you, Ahmed." John handed him a couple of *rials*. "Until next time. *Khuda Hafiz*." With a wave at Steve, he walked toward the Land Cruiser and climbed in. Leaning over, he planted a kiss on Adriana's cheek.

"Everything okay, *habibi?*"

"Yes, my darling," Adriana smiled.

"Good, let's go." He started the engine and backed out of the tire shop and with a wave at Ahmed, pulled out onto the street.

"Wait, can you stop at the petrol pump? I want some snacks for the journey."

"Sure." John pulled over and watched as Adriana climbed out and walked toward the shop, her long black hair swinging from side-to-side in a high ponytail, the shape of her figure still evident despite her loose linen clothing. He waited until she went inside, then reached into his pocket and pulled out Bogdan's iPhone. Scrolling through the contact list, he found the number he wanted, then tapped on video call and waited. The phone rang as he kept one eye on Adriana through the glass of the shop window. It was answered on the second ring, appearing on the screen a face he had hoped he'd never see again.

"Surya Patil."

Surya Patil's mouth dropped open in shock.

"Yes, I bet you didn't expect to see me. Now, listen carefully. I'm coming to get you, you bastard." John leaned closer to the screen. "How dare you come after me! Your son got what he deserved. He killed my wife." John glanced up toward the shop before continuing, "It was supposed to end there, but now, I'll hunt you down and make you suffer so much, you will wish you were dead with your son."

The door of the shop opened, and Adriana stepped out with a plastic bagful of snacks. John ended the call, switched off the phone and slipped it back into his pocket. Leaning across, he opened the door for Adriana and took the shopping bag from her hand as she climbed in, smiling at her.

"Ready?"

"Did you call him?"

"I did."

"Good," she replied with a grin. *"Yalla, habibi!"*

ALSO BY MARK DAVID ABBOTT

Book 5 Coming Soon

Have you read the other books in the John Hayes series?

Vengeance - John Hayes #1

When a loved one is taken from you, and the system lets you down, what would you do?

John Hayes' life is perfect. He has a dream job in an exotic land, his career path is on an upward trajectory and at home he has a beautiful wife whom he loves with all his heart.

But one horrible day a brutal incident tears this all away from him and his life is destroyed.

He doesn't know who is to blame, he doesn't know what to do, and the police fail to help.

What should he do? Accept things and move on with his life or take action and do what the authorities won't do for him?

What would you do?

Vengeance is the first novel in the John Hayes series.

Available now on Amazon

A Million Reasons: John Hayes #2

John Hayes is trying to move on but it's not easy.

Haunted by nightmares after the death of his wife he attempts to start a new life in Hong Kong, but the excitement and glamour of the city soon wears off and he finds himself deep in a rut. A mental state bordering on depression, a job he hates, and a salary that fails to last til the end of the month.

Until one day he finds a million dollars in his bank account!

It could change his life forever, but.....it comes with dangerous strings attached. Once again he is tested. Should he keep the money, break the law and potentially turn his life around, or should he give it all up and continue with his unhappy depressing existence?

Just how far is he willing to go?

What would you do?

What people are saying about "A Million Reasons"

"A great read, definitely worthy of 5 Stars. Written by a true wordsmith who knows how to draw his readers in to an exciting story with a number of unexpected twists."

"The second book in the John Hayes series is even better than the first!!"

Available now on Amazon.

A New Beginning: John Hayes #3

A chance meeting with a fascinating woman has the potential to change John's life. Could she be the one to bring him the happiness he lost after his wife was brutally murdered?........ Will it be that easy?

Newly wealthy John Hayes is living an idyllic life in the exotic city of Bangkok. He spends his days keeping fit, exploring the city and enjoying the wonderful food but he is lonely,........and when a beautiful woman walks into his life he thinks he has a chance to start afresh.

But with John life is never simple.

A penniless young girl desperate to start a new life..........a high flying foreign businessman with a murky past.......an alluring woman....... all come together to test John once again. Should he get involved and potentially risk his life and the lives of others? Or should he walk away and lose the woman he is growing to love?

"Great Book. Captivating. Well written and with enough suspense along with a bit of romance that keeps you turning the pages."

Available now on Amazon.

READY FOR THE NEXT ADVENTURE?

The next book is currently being written, but if you sign up for my VIP newsletter I will let you know as soon as it is released.

Your email will be kept 100% private and you can unsubscribe at any time.

If you are interested, please visit my website:

www.markdavidabbott.com
(No Spam. Ever.)

ENJOYED THIS BOOK? YOU CAN MAKE A BIG DIFFERENCE.

First of all thank you so much for taking the time to read my work. If you enjoyed it, then I would be extremely grateful if you would consider leaving a short review for me on the store where you purchased the book. A good review means so much to every writer but especially to self-published writers like myself. It helps new readers discover my books and allows me more time to create stories for you to enjoy.

ACKNOWLEDGMENTS

I would like to thank the following:

My friends, Sophie and Mathias for your input on the French language.

Zuwainah, for all things Omani, including your incredible hospitality.

Warka, Fay, and Shams, for your help with Arabic.

My editor Sandy Ebel - Personal Touch Editing, as always, without you I would have an unreadable manuscript. Angie-O e-Covers once again provided a cracking cover.

Last but not least, my long suffering wife, K. Thank you for tolerating my mood swings as I ride the roller coaster of emotions that make up a writer's life.

ABOUT THE AUTHOR

Mark can be found online at:
www.markdavidabbott.com

on Facebook
www.facebook.com/markdavidabbottauthor

on Instagram
instagram.com/thekiwigypsy

or on email at:
www.markdavidabbott.com/contact

- facebook.com/markdavidabbottauthor
- instagram.com/thekiwigypsy

Printed in Great Britain
by Amazon